To all my friends who, at one point or another over the last five years, took the time to read this book and encouraged me to get it out into the world, I can't thank you enough.

Thank you in particular to Rachel for your endless enthusiasm, to Iestyn for your amazing words of support, and to Laura for your continuous motivation, incredible generosity, and for all the Burns Nights at which I was allowed to perform many an excerpt!

Thank you also to my sister, Fiona, for attempting to spellcheck my mess of a first draft. And lastly, thank you to my wonderful wife, Anna, for always being there no matter what, and to my mum and dad, to whom I owe everything.

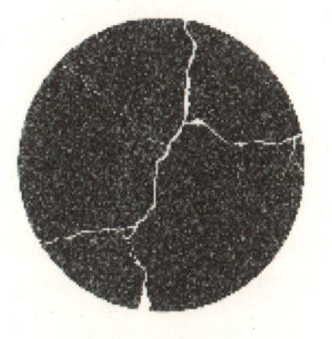

TROUBLE IN SPIRITLAND

paul tinto

TAB'S HOUSE

Copyright © 2024 Paul Tinto

The moral right of the author has been asserted.

All rights reserved.

No part of this publication may be reproduced, stored in a retrieval system, or transmitted, in any form or by any means, without prior permission in writing of the author, nor be otherwise circulated in any form of binding or cover other than that in which it is published and without a similar condition including this condition being imposed on the subsequent purchaser.

All characters and events in this publication are fictitious and any resemblance to real persons, living or dead, is purely coincidental.

Book Cover by Madison Coby

A CIP catalogue record of this book is available from the British Library

First published in 2024

Excerpts first performed live in 2019

ISBN 978-1-7384707-0-9

Published in Great Britain

Imprint - Tab's House Press

For more information:
contact@tabshouse.com
contact@troubleinspiritland.com

CHAPTERS

CHAPTER I	2
CHAPTER II	10
CHAPTER III	15
CHAPTER IV	24
CHAPTER V	25
CHAPTER VI	30
CHAPTER VII	43
CHAPTER VIII	50
CHAPTER IX	60
CHAPTER X	68
CHAPTER XI	82
CHAPTER XII	90
CHAPTER XIII	96
CHAPTER XIV	106
CHAPTER XV	108
CHAPTER XVI pt. I	116
CHAPTER XVI pt. II	140
EPILOGUE	151

Curiosity's Truth	*45*
Hate's Promise To Death	*52*
Hate's Prayer	*59*
I Knew Love Once, Back In A Happier Day	*73*
You Are He	*77*
Hate's Call To The Downtrodden	*80*
The Death Of Reason	*89*
Compassion's Last Request	*103*
Blame	*110*
The Search For Home	*113*
Hate's Confession	*125*
Where Have You Been?	*133*
True Love's Will	*136*
The Journey Home	*143*

For Mum

*"Are we but shooting stars in the night
Or is our course mapped out in the sky?
In death will I learn the meaning of life
Or learn it was all a meaningless lie?
Was it all pre-made, this part I played,
Or did I choose my own evens and odds?
Or were my joys and pain
No more than chips in a game
Of roulette between Fate and the Gods?"*

CHAPTER I

In the early hours of the morning
He slipped out from the sheets
And quietly put on his clothes.
He glanced back at Love, sleeping, peaceful, serene
And what was going through his head, even he didn't know.
The curtains flowed in the gentle breeze
With the balcony doors ajar
Letting in the moonlight, softly glowing on her skin,
And the sounds of the city playing out from afar.
But even on this softest and gentlest of nights,
Where not even the clouds wanted to stir,
A tempest was growing within his mind.
In such times, we can't help
The confusing thoughts that occur.
And so, silently stepping towards the door,
So not to kill Love's dreams,
He turned the handle, slipped out,
Took one last look and, like closing a book,
Shut it behind him;
End of a chapter, or so it might seem.

With his eyes to the ground he wound through the streets
Taking turns onto alleyways with no light at the end;
Careless, reckless, thoughtless, unthinking,
When confusion is present we feel like we're sinking
Deeper and deeper into the unknown,

CHAPTER I

Where the garbage bags decay
In the same place they were thrown
Days ago, weeks ago, who cares -
You've strayed into the shadows where life and its wares
Settle with the scent of piss in the air.
Then, taking a turn onto another small street
He was greeted by Lust, standing clouded in the heat
Of the steam rising up from the vents beneath.
"What's the matter?" she said.
"You look troubled. Don't let your worries sit underneath
Your fragile heart, your gentle soul.
Let me take you to a place
Where your conscience takes no toll."
She held out her hand, he reached out to hers
And, knowing there's a place where sense won't occur,
He followed her blindly through the hidden door
To where strangers meet
And questions are asked no more.

Up the stairs and through the corridors he walked,
Seeing drapes covering doorways, for such visions are locked
To Curiosity - He has no place here.
Respect others' wishes, and the one rule to adhere to:
Not to wonder, or think, or judge goings-on;
Your only concern is the tune of your own song.
It's yours to play, and as Lust would say,
"Your concerns have no currency here.
Here, the night never meets the day."
Half awake, half in a dream, she led him up to room fifteen,
And with those final words she pulled aside the blinds
And there, glowing before him, was one of a kind.
Her innocence shone brightly through her big brown eyes

And though he didn't know,
It was Purity,
Young Purity on the bed, ready to die.
The blinds closed behind him, and alone, there they were -
Two strangers in time where Time has no care.
She leant back on the bed as she was taught
And he stepped towards her, knowing not
What the hell he was doing,
But he knew his desire -
"Can you take me away from the flames of the fire
Burning in my mind - for I can no longer see
Who I am, who I was, or who I should be.
I'm committed in life, and I think I want out
From the future troubles described by my friend, Doubt."
He stepped closer and closer,
The floorboards creaking,
And she watched him approach
Seeing eyes only seeking
A liberty, a freedom,
A change, a reason,
Validation and purpose
As we enter the next season
Of rain and cold;
The summer's grown old,
And we think towards the challenges
That the next winter holds.
"Shhhhh," she said, holding his hand -
Purity, a slave to the laws of the damned.
In a world like ours
We prey on the cowards,
Tearing off the petals from their soft, gentle flowers.
"What is your name?" she said,

CHAPTER I

In a voice gently spoken.
"My name is Fear, husband of Love," he replied,
In a voice that was weak, shaken, broken.
We need not describe what happened next
For our imaginations, movies and so many texts
Have so often depicted the dark world of
Passionate mistakes that can't be undone,
And sordid regrets that leave senses stunned.
Fear lay there naked, cold sweat on his back;
On the damp-stained ceiling he stared at the cracks
And felt dust sprinkle down on his cold, wet skin,
For the customer above was lasting longer than him.
He looked over at Purity, but those beautiful eyes
Seemed cold now as she slipped back on her dress;
So he tried to remember the feeling of her thighs
And get one last glance at those young, soft breasts.
"You're free to go," she said, as she tossed him a rag
To wipe away the deed that had just come to pass.

Purity: Lust will be waiting just down the hall
         And if you want to tip me,
         Leave some money in the glass.

He sat up on the bed, looked between his legs,
His dignity sagging, hiding, dimly lit,
So he pulled off the rubber, or what was left of it.
In the heat of the moment, the sheath had split.
"Fuck it,"
He thought, as he tossed it away,
"What happens here dies here and never sees day."
Then he put on his jeans, walked straight out the door,
And left his future and dignity lying dead on the floor.

Down the corridor stood Lust, cigarette in hand.
"Relax," she said,

Lust: Nothing is planned
        In this world where saints
        Share the streets with the damned.
        Time and Chaos have been lifelong friends.
        Nobody knows what's real or pretend.
        You've come to a place where hearts want to mend.
        Those on the brink... Come now, this way,
        Let us pour you a drink.

And she led him downstairs, winding this way and that,
Deeper into the world, this underworld,
Where things simply try to survive.
Where the light bulbs flicker with their very last light,
Where the wallpaper clings to its very last paste,
Where bent nails age in rust,
Where the faeces of mice have dried up to dust,
Where the floorboards creak with rotting knots
Warped from the drips that have dripped for years
Like water torture. And so it seemed to Fear
He had found the place where no one can hear
Your confessions, obsessions, deep-seated depressions.
'What a place," he thought, *"where your only possession
Is your next choice to do as you please."*
And then into the bar, Lust led him with ease.
Into the stale, dank air
He walked towards the shelves of booze
And, like everyone else fleeing from Care,
Wanted to believe he had nothing to lose.
"Can I have something strong?" Fear asked.

CHAPTER I

"*I want to forget.*"
Then a pure, clear liquid poured into his glass
Designed to numb all sense of regret.
Hunched over, lost, he stared down through his drink
And on seeing his reflection he couldn't help but think
Of who he is, who he was, or who he should be;
In a full-topped glass, he saw a soul that was empty.
Then, staring deeper and deeper into that pool of unknown,
He thought back to Love, sleeping alone,
Back in the place he once called home,
Lying there, peaceful, serene.
"*What can I be to her?*" he thought,

Fear: *I'm less than a has-been.*
        What can one give Love
        When Love is so pure?
        What can one give Love
        When only Love can endure
        Temptation, Worry, the conversations of Doubt?
        Love knows what she is and what she's about.
        What can I give Love that she doesn't possess?
        While she sleeps, here I am at the Devil's address.
        Love should find love, not fear;
        I'm not worthy of Love and all she holds dear.
        Saints should live with saints,
        The damned with the damned.

And with that,
"*Salut.*"
Head back -
Slammed.
Then, "*Hit me again,*" he said to the air

And knocked back another as if no one was there.
"Hit me again," he said once more,
Then kicked back a third, same as before.

F: Hit me again.
Hit me again.
Don't hold back,
It's either real or pretend.
Hit me again.
Hit me again.
Here's to the world where time has no end.
Hit me again.
Hit me again.
Hit me again,
Hit me again!
Hit me again,
Hit me again,
Don't hold back,
It's either real or pretend!
Hit me again,
Hit me again!
Here's to the world where time has no end!
Where the music plays on deep into the night
And no one is woken by dawn's new light.
Here's to that wretch spewing up on the floor;
Here's to those lost to opium in room 264;
Here's to those betting on their very last cent;
Here's to the gamblers who came and never went;
Here's to the rats in the sewers and pipes;
Here's to the cockroaches and every other parasite
Feeding off life and giving nothing back;
Here's to life stretched out on the rack!

CHAPTER I

Here's to life that barely exists -
Vigour's passed out and Zeal's so pissed
He's being sucked off by Apathy
And it feels like bliss.
Here's to those the world doesn't miss.
Hit me again.
Hit me again.
Here's to life, real or pretend!
Hit me again.
Hit me again!
Sing with me all, my newfound friends!
Next round's on me, shots at the bar!
Band! Give us music! Let me hear the guitar!

And in raucous fashion a reel picked up
And everyone spun until they threw up their guts.
The music played on with a warbled cheer
That rang off the whisky jars and bottles of beer.
Then, *"Dance with me now!"* Guilt yelled to Fear
And they sucked each other's necks
And licked each other's ears,
And he blocked out the vision of his wife sleeping dear...
For one thing was certain...
Love was not here.

CHAPTER II

6.30 in the morning, hauling himself up
The endless flights of stairs
Onto the fifth floor,
Quietly treading his way through the corridor,
Fear creeps in,
Silent, so not to wake Love, still deep within her dream.
He takes off his clothes, throws them in the basket,
Sprinkles them with aftershave,
Hoping to mask it -
The stench of smoke,
The scent of Shame,
But no harm done, no one to blame
(And a hot enough wash might bring out the stains.)
Then he brushes his teeth to freshen his breath
Then brushes them again, for he can still taste death
At the back of his tongue:
The cigarettes, the beer,
The coke, the rum.
Then he rinses his mouth,
Spits in the sink,
Lifts his head,
His eyes wide, black as ink.
Anyone who's been there knows
There's no comfort to be found
In learning you're still high
When the new day comes around;

CHAPTER II

What's to follow is that slow painful comedown
As you try to hide your thoughts from the world
And try not to let your depression unfurl.
All you can do is let the day unfold
And try not to look into that deep black hole.
So he turns around,
Turns around to the shower,
Turns on the shower,
And without thinking, steps straight in -
The cold splash shocks every nerve on his skin...
And then gently warming up, he falls back into that
Heavy, deep, drunken coma,
Breathing out, releasing last night's aroma
Of sweat, of sex, of vomit, of weed -
The cocktail of sins and regrettable deeds.
Dead to the morning, he lets the water fall,
Asleep on his feet, forehead against the wall.

But in another room, something is rising.
Birds are singing, the light is shining,
The breeze blows fresh through the soft silk curtains;
And although in this world nothing is certain
We can always hope that the new day comes.
And so Love stirred,
Opened her eyes,
But to her surprise found nobody there next to her.
Strange... Strange way to start the day, feeling incomplete,
No one there sharing the bed sheets.
She gets up, first steps of the day,
Heads into the hall...
And there, from the bathroom, come the soft sounds
Like a waterfall.

So she goes into the kitchen and starts her daily routine,
Albeit, it would normally start clean
By waking up next to your loved one, feeling complete,
But, at least she knows he's there.
So, she puts the kettle on
And rinses out last morning's cafetière.
She puts the radio on
To casually hear how the weight of the world
Has shifted overnight,
What rights have been wronged,
What wrongs have become right -
Or at least getting there, but normally not quite...
Not yet.
(But Love, she's the type
That will never give up hope for the good fight.)
Anyway, back to breakfast -
Love keeps it simple and plain - some fruit, some toast,
Some porridge at most;
None of these new age, western delights -
Smashed avocado on pumpkin seed bread
With a side pot of cashew butter
(In an awkward shaped jar
Which means you can't reach the dregs),
With a dash of lemon, mint on top,
Served on a slate or some impractical rock,
With a kale and ginger smoothie, dashed with turmeric,
The latest superfood, Super-Vit Bullet -
At least that's what we've been told.
There'll be a new diet when that one grows old...
But as new fads come and new fads go,
Porridge seems to remain.

CHAPTER II

It's comforting to think that some things might always just
Stay the same...
(Nobody here is pulling porridge from the breakfast game.)
And then there he was,
Looking somewhat fresher than before;
Fear stood there at the door
In his dressing gown, towel around his neck.
Love smiled as if she hadn't seen him for days
In that kind of smile that seems to say
'Now I'm excited about today,
Now that you're in it with me'.
"You're up early," she said.
He smiled, trying to hide the throbbing in his head,
And replied,
"So are you. I was going to bring you breakfast in bed."
And it was there and then,
That was when he crossed a line
And forever said goodbye to a simpler time.
Up until that point, he could have confessed,
Said what had happened, and admitted the mess
He'd created - the stress, the worries, the confusion,
Admitted his mistakes and the cracks he'd made
In the tectonic plates of their relationship,
To try and communicate and so steady the shakes
Before the earthquakes force foundations to break
Beyond repair.
But that takes courage.
And Love hadn't married Courage. She'd married Fear.
And so, when that moment came,
Fear lied.
And he did it looking her right in the eye.

And she believed.
And why would she not?
In kindness and trust was Love conceived.
Now, some might argue in such a family you're raised naive,
But in what world would you automatically assume
You're being deceived?
In actual fact, that world does exist.
It weaves through the tapestry
Of both your world and mine.
It's the world where children have grown up and missed
Family support, a community,
The right to a fair and equal opportunity.
Why would you trust in a world where, your whole life,
You've been blamed for its failings?
Where, in your society, you've been neglected;
Your mayor is Privilege and he's been elected
Through his family and friends. His sole objective?
For his way of life to remain protected.
But the bitter irony is that Love had
Dedicated her life to eradicate
This world just described.
She believed, with the teachings of Selflessness,
Kindness and Trust can everyone thrive.
Yet, now her husband, her reason for being,
With a single lie
Was gambling with the faith
Love believed could never die.

CHAPTER III

That fateful day passed and nothing happened.
The next day came and same again.
In fact, it was a beautiful, calm, peaceful weekend -
It was almost like Time hadn't noticed.
But make no mistake, Time sees everything
And will join up all your dots in the end.
And in the night sky, the next generation
Can read every success, sorrow and joyful celebration
Of your life.
And so, Fear pushed through that day and managed to forget.
If you saw him you'd believe he had no regrets.
It's like when you're so hungover and you say,
"That's it. Never drinking again,"
And then...
Two days later you feel fine...
And with your dinner you treat yourself
To a wee glass of wine.
And just as that recovery becomes easy,
So do lies.
If you succeed in the first then you're cursed
And therein lies a relationship's demise.
And so, Time watched on, carefully disguised
As the butcher, the baker, the bus station caretaker,
Already knowing of what was to come
And what was worse, he knew nothing could be done -
That Future's hands were tied.

But life carried on as usual for Love and Fear,
Paying with the daily grind for the things you hold dear:
You wake up, have breakfast, kiss each other goodbye,
Go to work, make it to the gym,
(Or not),
Think towards the evening and what you've got
For dinner,
Or any plans you've made;
Come back home,
Relax,
See each other again,
Talk about your day,
Watch TV,
Let your mind wander to tomorrow
And what your future might be;
And all the while you forget that, silently,
Time is sitting there, holding the key to the shackles
That keep you chained to this world.
But even in such a prison, we're still able to feel,
To live,
To take and to give,
And then to feel again in that giving -
To feel in giving, that's living.
At least that's what Love lived for -
To give.
And she gave to Fear;
She gave to Fear everything she held dear
And in return, he gave her purpose.
And so, even in that daily routine
And everything in between -
The finance, the bills,

CHAPTER III

The insurance policies and wills,
The cooking, the cleaning,
Everything you've been meaning to
Redo, remend, the meaningless tasks that have no end -
All of these things you happily take
Because the reward comes in the happiness you make
With the moments Time has given you together
To use as you please;
Whether it's a holiday, a movie, or just shooting the breeze,
Eating together, putting the world to rights,
Imagining your fantasy world -
Where you have that and they have this -
And your careless laughter turns into a kiss,
And you hold each other close, so close.
Out of it all, this is what you enjoy the most;
Feeling wanted, feeling together,
That feeling where you think this will last forever.
You're not even scared
And you happily leave yourself unprepared
For what is to come when the light seems to fade...
When the darkness sets in from the choices you made.
And so it seeps in, slowly, subtly, invisible to the eye.
Time, though he may seem ruthless, is never in a rush
To deal out the cards that will hurt so much.
Often he gives us all the chances he can
To change our course.
But Fear being Fear, did nothing.
Weeks turned into months and things changed.
You don't know what at the start, it's hard to explain.
It begins with the odd day where there's no kiss goodbye
And then on return, your greeting is no more than '*Hi.*'

Then the conversation gradually gets less,
And although Love would try her best
To chat about their day,
It seemed like Fear didn't have much to say.
Then, in the evenings, while watching TV,
Silence is the presence in the room.
He's like a friend you said could crash for a night or two
But a week later he's still there,
Settling in, sunk into the armchair.
But Love, with Love's patience,
Would never ask him to leave,
Even at the point when it was hard to breathe.
She carried on, trying to get through
To the husband she loved and believed she knew.
But it was plain to see, something had shifted;
Two lovers that seemed to have drifted apart at sea,
A sea cold, dark and blue;
Two strangers, like ships passing in the night,
Each of them their own one-person crew
Trying to navigate waters unknown.
And that horrible feeling that nothing seems right
Is confirmed when, in bed,
You switch off the light
And you no longer kiss one another goodnight.
You turn over and hold tight to your feelings of sorrow
And fall asleep to the thoughts
Of what might come tomorrow.

It went on for months;
Love was lost, confused.
And so was Fear

But Fear also knew,
He just didn't know what to do.
And while Love was left to worry and guess,
Fear did what Fear does best:
Nothing.
And although Love could feel something was wrong,
Fear didn't let it show.
Over time, he'd become a pro
At perfecting his lies,
Hiding the truth that sat behind his eyes.
Eventually, he felt nothing. He kept no friends;
He blocked the numbers of Concern and Guilt
And kept himself to himself with walls built
So strong, you wondered if he even knew right from wrong.
And Love continued to guess and worry,
And worry and guess,
And worry some more, taking therapy with Stress,
Trying to figure out where her other half had gone.
And then, one Sunday afternoon,
Out of nowhere, with all she had left,
She took in a sharp, quick breath,
"What's going on?" she asked...
In that moment she knew there was no going back.
All that was heard was the faint tick...tock,
Tick...tock, tick...tock of the clock;
Time, a spectator with front row seats
To this moment where Present and Future would meet.
"What do you mean?" Fear replied,
Frowning, smiling confusion to hide his eyes.
Love breathed in, trying to steady the nervous sensation;
She had never been good at confrontation.

Love: *I mean…what's going on with you? With us?*
I feel like our relationship is on the cusp of ruin
And I don't know why.
I feel like I am living with a stranger
And I don't know why.
It feels like my marriage is about to die
And my husband isn't here to help me save it.
I am standing in the eye of a storm
And I have tried to brave it
But I don't know if I can anymore.
Where have you gone? What's on your mind?
What are you thinking?
I've been trying to reach out but I feel like I'm sinking
Deeper and deeper into the unknown.
Where do you go when the light's fading?
Where do you go when it all becomes so degrading?
I can't reach you anymore.
Have we drifted so far apart?
I can no longer feel the pulse of your heart.
Let me in, let me in.
Please, let me feel the warmth of your skin.
I know you have pain growing deep inside
And although you say you're fine,
It's impossible to hide;
I can see your grief and feel your sorrow
Of every today and every tomorrow.
I fall asleep at night holding onto my prayers
Hoping you know that I'm here and I care
But you need to let me in. Let me in.
Let me feel the warmth of your skin.
Or is it me? Is it me –

CHAPTER III

Am I the cause of your misery?
If so, don't conceal your dagger
In a sheath of kindness,
For only in honesty can Courage find us and
Give us the strength to fight the pain that Future holds;
Only in honesty can we both save our souls.
Just tell me.
Whatever the colour of the blood in your heart,
Just tell me.
Whatever the pain we may have to endure,
Just tell me.
I live with questions and no answers
And with that, Fear, it grows like a cancer.
So please, just tell me.
Let me in, let me in,
Let me feel the warmth of your skin.

Suddenly, like a supersonic sound
Shattering the glass between them,
The doorbell rang.
For the first time in months
They stood present in the same room,
Though neither knew the impending doom
That awaited on the other side of the door.
Fear's feet were rooted to the floor.
Love wasn't expecting anyone.
Time waited, and watched...
Almost in slow motion Fear reached for the handle...
Gripped it...
Turned it...
Pulled it...

The slight creak of the hinge echoed in the air...
And there stood a young spirit, barely seventeen years of age
But for the grease in her hair,
And the bags hanging heavy under shadowed lids,
And her cheekbones, like cliff edges, ready to give,
Curving over the caves of her jaw,
So malnourished she was beyond even Poverty's law.
The deep lines, like canyons in her skin,
Ploughing all the way down to her weathered core within,
Told stories no one should have to read, let alone live;
Seventeen years of age but for all those
Who had had their wicked way
And ravaged her youth.
Fear looked into those hazlenut brown eyes,
Her beauty's final refuge.
There was no mistaking the spirit he recognised
From that night eight months before:
It was Purity, young Purity, standing there at the door.
And from that worn face
That makeup could no longer conceal
He glanced down to her stick-thin neck,
To her stick-thin arms,
To her twig-thin wrists,
To her leaf-veined hands
That cradled a round, swollen,
Unmistakable bump beneath her dress.
There, sleeping inside Purity, was the truth
Fear could never confess to Love.
And as Fear looked to Purity, while Purity looked to Love,
While Love looked to Fear,
Everything to everyone became abundantly clear.

CHAPTER III

Then Fear did what Fear can only do
When Fear has nothing left:
He ran.
He bolted and ran.
The coward inside him that hides deep within man
Went rushing through his veins,
Like a deserter on the run being hunted by Shame.
Fear ran, leaving Purity, Love, and a child unborn -
A sight which Time and Future would mourn.
There they stood, silent, two spirits sharing the same air,
Breathing in the same vapour of despair
Deep into their lungs
While, in the heavens, by the choir of angels,
In darkening discord their dirge was sung.
"May the Gods forgive me for the damage I've done,"
Purity spoke, then vanished from the door.
Love tried to speak but was paralysed to her core,
Tried to take a step then buckled to all fours.
Her life was shattered.
In a single moment, Love had lost everything she held dear,
While the world sat pregnant with the son of Fear.

CHAPTER IV

Things changed in SpiritLand after that day.
But when cracks in the land
Don't affect where we stand
So often we choose to turn the other way
And too easily forget the simple truth
Written into the constitution of Life:
That we are all connected,
And if another's pain we leave neglected
We will suffer in the coming of Strife.

Love knew this truth,
But who looks out for Love
When Love learns she's not bulletproof?
When we cover our ears and close our eyes,
Hoping someone else hears the inconsolable cries,
Silence is made by passive uncaring,
And in that silence, one spirit hears
The tune of despairing.
And thus, Grief appeared, as Grief does,
Uninvited into Love's home.
He didn't say how long he would stay,
He just disconnected the phone
And then pulled a cloud across the sky,
Pitching it perfectly above;
And in the shadow's sphere did they both disappear,
Grief, and his new captive, Love.

CHAPTER V

And in the weeks thereafter the skies got darker
As if the weather was turning a rage;
Something was breaking, something was waking,
Rattling Contentment's cage.
Winds blew with reckless abandon,
Tearing their way up the streets,
Whirling up trash, out on the lash,
Smashing glass off the concrete.
Smoke billowed into the air,
Cars were set alight,
Oil cans burned and the underworld learned
How to let darkness glow bright.
Baseball bats shattered shop storefronts,
Shelves were pillaged and robbed,
Chaos danced drunk on a mountain of junk
Conducting the chants of the mob:

Chaos: *Let him come,*
        He is The One,
        He is The One, our Chosen Son.
        Let him come,
        He is The One,
        He is The One, our Chosen Son.
        Let him come,
        For all that's been done,
        Let him come, our one True Son.

> *Let him come,*
> *He is The One,*
> *He is The One - The Chosen Son!*

And they wound their march
Through the backways and alleyways,
Searching for the stable where their Mother Mary lay.
And at the back of a block where the righteous ignore,
With boarded-up windows and boarded-up doors,
In a guest house for junkies and a refuge for whores,
Purity, in labour, bled out on the floor.
She breathed and she sighed,
She moaned and she writhed,
Gripping Lust's hand as she wretched out a cry.
She squeezed and she pushed,
Doing all that she could,
As her feet found their grip in splinters of wood.
"Let him come!" the crowds chanted.
"LET HIM COME!" the crowds ranted!

> *Let him come,*
> *He is The One,*
> *He is The One, OUR ONE TRUE SON!*

And while the chants you could hear
Far and clear,
Way out at the bridge
Where the drunks sleep with beer,
Trembling in fright, was our old friend, Fear,
Rocking back and forwards, covering his ears.

F: *What have I done, what have I done?*

CHAPTER V

Please don't give birth to my one true son.
What have I done? Gods, don't let him come!
Please don't give birth to my one true son.

But back at the inn,
Where no shepherds or kings
Or old wise men would dare venture within,
The booze is flowing, the crowds are growing,
Waiting to hear of news that she's showing.
Purity spasms, she kicks, she screams;
The vents in the alleyways puff scorching steam;
The breath of the ground panting and shaking,
The womb of the earth with a force in the making
Too strong to hold back.
Purity contracts.
The ground starts to crack!
The soil bleeds out blood pure black.
The drums of thunder rolled over the plains
Preparing its offering of fire and rain.
Rivers rose and flooded their banks
And flowed down the streets preparing their thanks.
Icebergs crumbled, oceans roared,
Lightning bolts struck the earth to its core.
Then Purity howled up the pain from her gut
As new life tore wounds from all the times she'd been fucked
By Loneliness, Jealousy and all of the rest -
Guilt, and Fear, whom she'd come to detest!
And with rage and anger burning inside
She drove out the being with full force of the tide...
And then there he was...
Life's new creation,
Which Purity held with an overwhelming sensation,

One strange and new;
That your purpose in life is no longer you
But the child in your arms,
Whom you promise upon your heart will never see harm.
But that's not in your control -
Only the Gods have the say for our souls.
But even they looked down upon this child unsure;
The son of Purity, no doubt he was pure,
But pure in what?
In his eyes lay a darkness tempered and hot.
Then the sounds of his cries made the junkies rise
From their lonely slumber and loathing demise.
While outside, the downtrodden soon heard of the news
And with meaningless alms, processed in their queues.
The winds blew cold, the sky turned dark,
Paranoid dogs growled and barked.
And though rejoicing could be heard,
Future knew we would mourn;
For in this darkest of nights,
Hate had been born.

*"Are we but shooting stars in the night
Or is our course mapped out in the sky?
In death will I learn the meaning of life
Or learn it was all a meaningless lie?
Was it all pre-made, this part I played,
Or did I choose my own evens and odds?
Or were my joys and pain
No more than chips in a game
Of roulette between Fate and the Gods?"*

CHAPTER VI

Way out beyond the back end of town,
Where birdsong is drowned out by siren sound,
Is a world forgotten,
Where the high street is a graveyard
For the small man's business.
Where once work flourished
Now dreams are malnourished,
Being starved by the chains and the big corporate names
Which grow gluttonously fat on their profit.
Where once was inspiration, now there's barely aspiration,
For who would aspire to shop-front degradation?
Who would aspire to the deepening humiliation
Of having no job?
To stand on your feet knowing you can make ends meet
And pay your way from day to day,
For so many, gives reason for being;
For not everyone has the fortune of existence so freeing
As living for someone else,
Sparing you from justifying your life to yourself.
And in this slum of a town
With its buildings run down,
Where Poverty drinks the water turned brown,
There's a small basement flat hidden from the light.
It's not much, it's not even enough.
Still, it's better than sleeping rough
When you have a child to raise

CHAPTER VI

And it's all Charity had to offer
In these darkening days.
And so, within these damp rotten walls,
With an air of sewage lingering in the hall,
Resided Purity,
Burning incense sticks of hope to try and freshen the air,
Scraping by as best she could so the cupboard wasn't bare.
Her comfort at night? The solace of prayer.
And there, in that flat, did she raise Hate,
With all the devotion and care a mother could give a child.
An old mattress, moth-eaten and stained, was their bed.
His toys were planks of wood and old pipes of lead.
His night-time stories? Whatever was in Mum's head;
Myths of Providence,
Praying to the Gods she wasn't dead.
And Purity did what any loving single mother would;
She raised her child as best she could,
Taking any help she could get from the neighbourhood -
For even Poverty still has a heart that beats.
Charity would come round and help Purity rest her feet,
And when she was too tired and could no longer
Hush the baby's cry,
Patience would pop by
And rock Hate to sleep in her arms.

Patience: If only these innocent eyes you could keep
        And not witness the suffering
        That makes worn eyes weep;
        But the purity of the spirit,
        As delicate as a butterfly's wing,
        Is too fragile to withstand the sins that we bring.

And so, from cradle to crawl
To football against the wall!
Hate wore his team's strip from
Dawn through to nightfall -
A kit for which his mum had saved
Months worth of a wage
Just to see her son happy
In his innocent young age.
There he was, wearing number 10,
And in that shirt, he would win World Cup
After World Cup
After World Cup,
Again and again and again.
Each time, in the dying seconds of the game,
He'd go it alone - always the same -
Past one player, two players, three players, four,
Then BANG!
Watch the ball soar
Towards the postage stamp corner........GOAL!
He's done it again! You couldn't ask for more!
What a time to be alive -
Life is great at the age of five.
And Purity would watch her young one play
Whenever she wasn't working...
But she was working nearly every single day -
One job, two jobs, three jobs, four,
Endlessly trying to afford a life for her child
That was better than the one he'd been born into.
She worked as a cleaner, she worked as a waitress,
Countless interviews for the role of receptionist.
At night she handed paper towels out
In fancy toilets of pretentious bars

CHAPTER VI

Hoping for tips to fall into her jar,
Then onto the early-doors shift
At the desolate 24-hour petrol station -
Anything she could to help build her reputation
And save that of her child - that was more -
She wouldn't let the world brand him the son of a whore.

But back on the street
Hate became a popular kid,
Calling out the games while others copied what he did.
He and Pride Jr were best of friends,
Looking like they'd be friends to the end;
Two wee wise guys shooting wits and gags,
Pride dreaming of riches, standing in his rags.

Pride: *I'll be something some day Ms P, you'll see.*
Just you watch,
It's only a matter of time
On that piece of shit clock.
No one's gonna tell me what I can and can't do -
Not in this life.

Two little tearaways, not bad kids, just lively and happy,
Killing time playing dares and chappy,
Driving Discipline and Rage out of their flats,
Onto the streets with baseball bats
Calling, *"I'll fucking find you, you cuntin' wee brats!"*
All harmless fun, just being themselves
At seven or eight, or even twelve;
At least for Immaturity that was the case -
That young kid just never seemed to grow up.

But then, as the years go on,
These fun and games get left behind,
Back up the street in a different time;
The football abandoned by the gate,
Wedged in at the hinges, left to slowly deflate
Like that five-year-old's dreams -
You're a different kid at the age of fifteen.

There he is, no longer kicking a ball,
Just casually leaning against the wall,
Knowing it all:
Smoking, joking, wee bit of toking,
Hands in pockets, looking cool,
Making sure no one takes you for a fool -
For reputation is the golden rule
In surviving the lion's den
That is high school.
Sink or swim;
Watch yourself or get a doin' in the gym.
Basketball to the face -
Know your place -
School was a tough time for Meekness and Grace,
While Anarchy's kid, he was just a headcase,
Constantly on the prowl for stuff to deface.
But Hate, Hate was different. He just looked on,
Constantly questioning what was right and wrong,
Questions going round and round in his head,
Something bubbling underneath,
Something making him grind his teeth.
He'd push the boundaries,
Get the odd detention here and there,
But like most usual suspects he didn't really care.

CHAPTER VI

He started hanging out with a different crowd,
With Anger and Rebellion, who, like Pride, were proud.
And, in time, a different type of cloud
Formed over Hate;
The questions inside him started to grate.
He would look around at his class peers and think,
"What the hell am I doing here?"
Vanity sitting there checking his hair,
Insecurity trying to push up her breasts,
Ego's swinging back on his chair
While Ambition's about to fail another test.
Worry's got twenty rubbers on hand
While Ignorance is pretending he clearly understands
What the hell is being said
About algebra and equations - if X and Y equal Z.
Pride's necking Modesty in the girls' toilet,
Conspiracy's getting stoned in the janitor's closet.
Blame's grassing up Honesty for setting off the alarm,
Deceit's backing him up with her usual charm.
And Scandal's fucking anything he sees,
While his girlfriend, Faith, is completely naive.
Everyone tries to tell her, *"You're being taken for a ride!"*
But the idiot she is, she won't leave his side -
Pause.
As if watching, from the pews, a doomed future bride,
Hate began to see how it was.
He was sitting in a classroom,
Taught by the young niece of Hope,
In a town where dreams are lit and go up in smoke
To help warm the homeless on the coldest of nights.
Say what you like about Hate, Hate was bright;
Constantly questioning why he was here,

Thinking about things way beyond his years.

Teacher: Can you answer the question Hate?
Hate: Why?
T: Excuse me?
H: Why?
T: Why?
H: Yeah, why?
T: Why what?
H: Why what? Is that the best you've got?
    Why answer the question?
T: Because I'm asking you to.
H: And I'm asking you what's the point?
T: Because it's part of your learning, your education.
H: My education?
    Now there's a problem with no fucking equation,
    Ay Miss?
    My education equals what?
    Dreams of jobs I'll never get?
    Scraping into university to scrape out with debt?
    We'd be so lucky.
    How much would you bet this means nothing at all,
    That we're all better off being shot against the wall?
    Or is that not an option?
    Are we too valuable for those that make a fortune
    Out of the growth industry that is
    'Societal Problem Solving',
    Being paid to build projects aimed at resolving
    The issues of communities in dire straits
    While still making sure it's left a dump of a place?
    Was this your dream Miss,
    To teach us in this shit hole?

CHAPTER VI

Or is this what you've settled for
After you didn't reach your goal?
You want your question answered?
Well, answer me this:
Why is Aspiration falling asleep?
Why has Progress thrown her jotters in a heap?
Why has Concentration shoved a pencil in his ear
And made himself deaf?
And while we're at it, our star pupil, Potential,
Her last grade was an F!
Perseverance is persevering at being a dick.
Endurance can't do a bleep test
Without making himself sick.
Aggression's suspended, Violence is expelled
Yet the playground is still a bloodbath
At the lunchtime bell.
Self-Assurance is bulimic, wee Angst is a smoker,
And he's now buying cigarettes
For the kid of Composure since the nutcase flipped,
While Anxiety sells him pills
She got after her old dear was laid off
For being mentally ill.
Stress has been silent since her dad was let loose
And what's worse, her mum's ditched him
For the bed of Abuse;
Apparently he's flush and he pays her way,
She just has to fuck him and
Take a beating twice a day.
Obesity's just another fat kid like many
But he's bullied for his sweets
For which he saves every penny;
Then you'll find him at lunchtime,

In tears over his third box of fries
As he comforts his shame for being so oversized.
Meanwhile, outside, Malnourishment looks on
But she can't stomach the irony
Of the fat kid's sad song.
See Good Will?
Her family's broke. Sympathy's is in debt.
Generosity got out when Altruism left.
And why is there loads of chewing gum under my desk?
Was that Disrespect
Or the lazy-arsed community service job of Neglect
After he left the kid that broke his neck?
And why, on my chair, does it say
'You're going nowhere'?
Who scored that there?
And where are they now?
And why do I get the sense they were right somehow?
I'll get my grade, you'll get paid,
But let's face it Miss, my future's already made
By Privilege and the rest of those private school lads
Who'll rise to the top with the help of their dads.
Why are they not in the clothes I wear?
Why is Envy right when she says this isn't fair?
Why is my glass ceiling a stained basement flat
Holding up six storeys ready to collapse,
Sitting there empty but for the junkies and drunks
That flock there aplenty for their Friday night rave -
The escape from Reality that everyone craves.
Disgust's on eccies once more feeling cleansed
Of self-hating thoughts he can't otherwise transcend,
While Concern's back on benzos living the dream
Of who she could be if she had self-esteem.

And in the back room,
Anguish and Agony have scored Heavenly Blue;
It's not quite love, but it's the best they can do.
A delusional party on the very top floor,
Believing it's a mansion
While they knock on Death's door;
But back again they go for their Friday night rave
While the kids wait on corners
As is the way to behave.
And so the cycle goes:
Performed by the parent, picked up by the child
And nurtured for adulthood to see them stay wild.
Hanging around the edge of the overgrown park -
You're either buying or selling
If you're there after dark.
You know those two old swings broncoed to shit?
Tolerance sells meth there, just doing his bit.
Self-Loathing's on the street necking cheap white wine
In a broken phone box that's dead to the helpline;
She's been married to the bottle since her husband left
And now offers couples threesomes
For the price of a cigarette.
And so, through the wall, her daughter ponders
On the weird, discomforting sounds of sex.
Contempt's got it in for Resilience and Grit,
Conscientiousness, Diligence,
And whoever else he sees fit;
They're a flat full of immigrants two blocks across
Getting racist death threats sent through the letterbox.
And while everyone else is fighting for scraps
Condemnation's just sitting back
To watch the show,

For she's bored of the rhetoric nobody wants to know.
Yet, Resistance? Somehow he's still here,
In the same damp place he's coughed in for years!
He can't get a job,
No money in the meter,
His flat's a retirement home
For lightbulbs and heaters.
He hasn't got a bank,
Can't afford a phone,
Couldn't call the ambulance
When he collapsed at home.
His bones are knackered, he can barely walk -
My mum picks up his benefits on her way to the shops
(I say shops, I mean food banks,
That joke of a system
For which I'm meant to give thanks!?)
He's been here so long he's seen it all:
From the closing of the library
To the opening of the shopping mall;
When the health centre shut,
When the community centre closed down,
He's seen the life of this town drown
In the floods of hardship and dysfunctional seas
As we cram onto a raft of misery and disease.
Even Morale's grown old
Worrying how long it will last.
So here we remain,
Anchored by the perception of the ruling upper class.
Yet, Resistance! He's still here!?
A victim of his strength,
While Scepticism makes a mint
Measuring coffin Lengths.

CHAPTER VI

So answer me this!
Why do politicians not visit our schemes?
Do they think we don't know what politics means?
Or do you think it's because they know all too well
That saving this place has no hope in hell?
So, again! You tell me of the education I need,
And for what? Wasn't I just born to bleed?
To bleed and to be bled
Like a pig stuffed and fed;
Told what to eat, told what to buy,
Just before I trot off to die
For the luxurious carvery of fat cats sitting high,
Who will dress up poverty's dry, chewy taste
Then sell it on above market rates.
You want the answer to your question?
I'll give it to you loud and clear.
It's sixty-six. Sixty-six years -
About double the life expectancy
For everyone here.
Why is that? Answer me that!
Actually, don't. Don't answer me that.
It's a waste of time,
Yours and mine.
You can teach their textbooks
But I won't be part of that crime.
So fuck it. Fuck all of it.
Fuck. This.
Fuck you Miss
And fuck this!
And before you say it, I know, I'm dismissed."

And that was that.

Didn't even wait to see
What the repercussions might be;
He just walked straight out the door,
Back to the streets, to his old familiar scene;
Hate left school at the age of sixteen.

CHAPTER VII

Time watched on as the years crept by.
From teens to twenties, Hate sharpened his eye
As he delved deeper into the shadows of his mind;
Who knows what you might find
When you stop looking for light
And your eyes adjust to the darkening sights
Of this world?
Curiosity led him down hidden streets,
The poverty porn tour where life and death meet,
With its scriptures sprayed on the wall:
*"What you don't know can't hurt you,
Yet, truth can set you free from it all."*
He led him down alleyways with no light at the end;
In darkness who knows what's real or pretend?
"Here is a place where hearts don't mend,"
Hate thought, as he kicked a garbage bag
Decaying with the rot of despair,
Releasing a scent of piss in the air.
Then suddenly, stopping by a ramshackle door,
"Wait... Why do I feel like I've been here before?"
As if Chance and Fate had been gambling pissed
With chips of truths, secrets and lies,
Hate stood outside, searching with his memory's eye,
While, on the other side of the door,
Two floors up, in room fifteen,
His mother was on her back in her old familiar scene.

In a last attempt to keep up with her rent
After losing her job when ill health came and went,
Purity returned to the trade that will always pay:
Selling fake love to keep heartache at bay.
And while her client, Denial, rode her raw,
Trying desperately to make himself come,
Purity had her eyes closed to it all,
Trying desperately to think of only her son,
Her only source of joy on this earth,
Who had unknowingly found the wasteland of his birth
And was now standing only thirty feet away -
Only a wall in between,
Separating the sorrows of the seen and unseen,
Dampening the sounds of the pain-felt screams.
"*What is this place?*" Hate asked,

H: *Why do I feel like I'm standing in my past?*
Why can I hear ghosts chanting my name
While the children of my imagination
Wield pitchforks and flames,
Ready to rise
Against a world that looked away and left us to die?
Why can I see angels with black wings?
Why can I hear those dark angels sing in discord,
Harmonising with the pain of my ancestors?
Why do I wish to torch the soil on which you stand
And release the underworld
To take arms with the damned
And wreak havoc across this so-called
Promised Land?
Who am I? Why am I here?
How can I see behind my youth so clear?

CHAPTER VII

Why do I sense that Truth resides near?

A shockwave pulsed through the sky.
Time held its breath.
The night hung still.
Denial's head lay on Purity's breasts
While Purity felt a cold air
Chill her to the bone.
Desire could feel Hate's presence stir;
"Could it be The Chosen Son has returned?"
Hate's eyes burned with a longing to know
What secrets lay behind the door.
"Lead me to Truth," Hate demanded.
But Curiosity stood there open-handed
And confessed,

*Curiosity's Truth

Curiosity: Through the hallways of our lives
There are rooms in which Truth bides
With doors on which I will never knock;
For once you find Truth, that door is locked
And the keys are in his possession.
Like the jailor, your friends are at his discretion -
You may walk free with Happiness,
He may leave you chained with Sadness
Who, in time, eventually morphs into Madness.
Truth is a ruthless creature;
He is the judge who cares not for saints or sinners,
He is the croupier who cares not
For losers or winners.
He does not answer to Justice,

He does not walk with Kindness,
He does not dine with Sympathy,
Nor give time to Pity.
He does not put trust in Faith,
He does not put faith in Trust.
There is one spirit for whom he will kneel in the dust
And that is Death -
For, despite all your distinction,
There is one ultimate truth:
No one will escape their final breath.
Truth is a dealer. That is his trade;
Making his money off the secrets we've made.
In the marketplace of Time,
Where Future sells to Present
And Present sells to Past,
Truth is there picking up every last scrap
Of what we haven't learned or collected,
What we've turned away from,
Or deceitfully neglected.
He will find you at unexpected moments
Further down the line
To lighten his load of what's yours or mine,
But when you search for him, that's when he profits
From the weight of the world he carries in his mind.
If you seek out Truth, you can not guarantee
What you'll find.
I have seen souls destroyed from what they have asked
After Truth turned over the cards of their past.
Some things are better off unlearned.

In nervous disquiet, Hate hovered over
Curiosity's line of caution drawn.

CHAPTER VII

Inside, Temptation whispered through the vents,
Calling his name, reaching out to his fame.
Enchantment, at the microphone, softly sang
Her luring tune which sweetly rang
Through every crack and every hole,
And the cuts of every wounded soul.
Desire sat in hopeful wait,
Bribery bought drinks at the bar for Fate.
*"Let him come, he is The One,
He is The One, our Chosen Son."*
Hate, half asleep, half awake,
Stared into the temple of pleasure...
But then stepped back.
The nerves in his mind sparked confusion and doubt,
The music cut out.

C: *Go home Hate.*
This is no place for one so young so late.

On hesitant heels, Hate turned and walked away.
Yet, all the while, from the shadows of the very top floor,
Thinking back to the baby she held years before,
Lust looked down upon the promised child.
While his mother lay bare in the sweat of Denial,
Lust's cold stillness warmed with a smile
As she watched him disappear into the darkness.
She knew she'd see him again.
For though the winds of life will cause trees to bend
Our roots run strong back into the earth
Whence we were born.

But for all the things that Lust could see

She could not have known how soon that would be;
For unknown to all, that night,
The Devil, in a moment of cruel delight,
Had spiked the life of Hate
With a joke that would seal Purity's fate
And send her son, wild and armed,
To seek revenge against his authors of harm.

"Are we but shooting stars in the night
Or is our course mapped out in the sky?
In death will I learn the meaning of life
Or learn it was all a meaningless lie?
Was it all pre-made, this part I played,
Or did I choose my own evens and odds?
Or were my joys and pain
No more than chips in a game
Of roulette between Fate and the Gods?"

CHAPTER VIII

And so, in the following months,
Back within the walls of their small basement home
Where Purity had raised her son with all that she owned,
Hate sat by his mother's bedside,
Helplessly watching a fever take hold.
Yet, while Purity turned hot to cold
Still she shone light into the room where shadows descended.
Like a rose stranded in winter snow, her beauty
Took each and every blow of pain with untempered serenity,
While behind her eyes,
The flickering and fading candle of life
Stubbornly refused to burn out and die.
"Just let me go," Purity prayed,
"Let me take the truths of my past to my grave."

What a cruel, twisted world is this,
Where a mother sells her body for the good of her son
In an act of love that will tear their love undone.
As if the Devil that past night had gotten Irony high
On a cocktail of drugs that sent him reaching for the sky,
Oh, how Satan laughed when he riddled Denial
With the wretched disease
That he thrust into Purity, prising open her knees.
Now she lies shivering, dying to leave
This wild west of takers and thieves,
Waiting, with each shallow breath;

CHAPTER VIII

How slow Time goes when one is waiting for Death.
"I'm cold," she weakly said.
Hate pulled up her blanket, felt her head,
Brushed back her soft brown hair,
And looked into those hazelnut brown eyes
That couldn't help but shimmer with innocence and grace,
Even on a sea of tears of unjust self-reproach.
Then, gently, her gaze drifted across the room
Before fixing on a lengthening rip and tear
That seemed to be splitting through the tapestry of the air.
And though, to Hate, nothing was there,
Purity was staring into a world beyond her own.
A warm breeze passed through her skin
As a figure appeared, standing within
A gateway to a valley of mesmerising hues,
Of emerald greens and electric blues,
Where purple shades of the glowing twilight
Blended with the yellows, reds and oranges of the sun;
A sky where night and day were one,
Where auroras seemed to wave like a parting sea,
Revealing a universe of stars like you wouldn't believe.
Purity smiled, reached out...
Then ceased to breathe.
...The air fell silent.
Hate held his mother's hand
Whose soul was now gone and gone forever.
Then, above the stillness of the air,
He sensed the presence of a spirit still lingering there.
"Hello Death," Hate said,
"Promise me this - in her next life you will give her rest
For in this world she was given none."
"I make promises to no one," Death replied,

"Only that I will find you when your time is nigh."
With eyes as cold as ice, Hate kept his back turned,
As if concealing a newfound disrespect for life.

*Hate's Promise To Death

H: *Well, hear my promise to you:*
You will see me again,
And again and again before my life meets its end.
You will see me in the fields,
You will see me in the cities,
You will see me at the executions
Of Forgiveness and Pity.
You will see me on the roads,
You will see me in the streets,
You will see me when Anarchy
Dances in the heat of the flames
As he burns alive those that are truly to blame
For all who have suffered
And been denied the right to be fathered or mothered.
You will see me at day, you will see me at night,
You will see me when Justice learns
Who is wrong and right;
At the spilling of blood, I will be in plain sight.
You will see me as Violence pummels Peace,
You will see me as the strength of Pride is unleashed
And lynches Dignity in front of the mob
While Grace and Honour are being raped and robbed.
You will see me in towns swarmed with mines,
You will see me as Kindness begs for more time.
As Righteousness stands at the altar of sin,
Absolving Nobility and Virtue within,

CHAPTER VIII

You will see me as Baseness twists his knife in
Through every back and every side
Of the congregation who pathetically hide
Behind a veil of goodwill.
You will see me when Compassion is killed
And the damned rise, led by Revenge,
In an army that will let Chaos descend.
Heaven's gates will lock for fear it will flood
And you, Death, will wade through a river of blood
That will soak through the soil into the world below
As wine for the demons getting drunk on the show
Of Hate -
The lives of Grief, Pain, and Poverty
Are not my fate.
This world has written the chapters of my youth
And those to blame will suffer -
So come forth and let me see you
Great Spirit of Truth.

CRACK!

Lightning bolts lit up the sky of black!
Truth awoke at the summoning of his name;
He could feel Hate bolting like a horse on free rein,
Drawing ever close.
Thunder rumbled from coast to coast.
Storm doors slammed and locked in fright,
Window shutters flapped in the wake of the night
While Hate was guided by flashes of light
Back to the alleyway that sat out of sight
To the rest of the world.
CRASH!

Hate hurled his weight at Temptation's door,
And smashed his way into the corridor -
Into the forgotten land of the addicts:
The addicts of sex,
The addicts of crack,
The addicts of booze,
The addicts of smack,
The addicts of grief,
The addicts of pain,
The addicts trying to hide from Shame.
And like everyone there, some force had Hate in its grasp,
Leading him past each horrid sight
More brutal than the last,
Past every string of beads and curtain drapes
Hiding sordid pleasures in twisted misshape:
Depravity masturbating while Beauty stripped,
Sadism laughing, cracking his whip,
Addiction helping Failure sleep
With a rusting needle scraping in deep.
But the force of Desire jolted Hate once more,
Pulling him up to the second floor,
Up through the damp, darkening halls
Of leaking pipes and graffiti-sprayed walls -
Fresh paint made the words drip and run:
"Let him come, for all that's been done,
Let him come, our one True Son."
And through this derelict wilderness of sights obscene
He led himself straight into room…
Fifteen…

A shadowed figure sat in the corner, half-lit,
While standing centre stage was Lust,

CHAPTER VIII

    Joy breaking through her painted face
    At the sight of her prince, come back to take his place.
    "Where am I?" Hate whispered, *"Why am I here?"*
    "Our son has returned after all these years!"
    Lust exclaimed.

Lu: *Oh, how you have grown.*
        You have turned into the spirit
        We have always known would rise
        And see the world through such hateful eyes
        That could give strength to the lives without reason.
H: *Who Am I?*
Lu: *You are he.*
        You were the birth the world came to see.
        The Anointed, The Famed,
        The Appointed, The Proclaimed.
H: *Hold your prophecy back in your heart!*

Hate took in his audience of two
As his voice started to seethe.

H: *I want answers. I know what I believe;*
        I wasn't brought onto this earth to grieve.
        So, Truth, if you are he, tell me straight -
        Give me my past in all of its weight.

    Truth sat there searching the burning eyes of Hate.

Truth: *Never underestimate the weight of this world,*
        Nor the difference between our beliefs
        And what we know to be true.
        Our beliefs we can carry

And then leave behind,
Or re-collect them, if we choose,
Further down the line.
But truths we take on from the moment we know
And will warp the branches
As your tree of conscience grows.

H: *My life has been warped by those that thieve*
The warmth of the sun to tan their own skin
While the rest shiver in the shadows!
My life has been written by those
Who turned their back
And let the downtrodden slip
So deep within the cracks
That my mother left this world as
Unnoticed as the dust in the air,
With such neglect and uncare
That, if not for Death,
She would have been left
To drag the soil of her grave
Over her own breasts.
So tell me, who am I?
Why am I here?
Show the cards of my past
And who is to blame for the dice that were cast?

There are some marbles of Knowledge
That even Truth would choose to leave
Forever enclosed in the darkness of their velvet purse;
For those swirling colours hold such magical powers
To curse the beholder who gazes into the stones'
Reflection in the cold light of day.
In that curse, the cursed curses another,

CHAPTER VIII

Who, in turn, curses our sister and brother,
And the chain of pain, in chinks of blame,
Grows and grows, shackling our ankles
As slaves of Destruction, who tear up the world
For no other function than to harvest the seeds of Rage.
But Truth isn't the maker of these marbles made,
Nor has the authority to refuse the buyer's request
Or choose what he thinks is for the best.
And so, setting his apprehension aside,
Knowing he had no power of the tides,
In a voice dead of emotion, he gave an answer
With words that would tempt the wake of Disaster:

Tr: *Between these four walls were you created*
While your mother gave pleasure
To those longing to be sedated
From the reality of their lives.
While Love lay asleep on a hot summer's night,
Her other half walked out
And, in broken winged flight,
Flew to this house of Temptation
Where, led by Lust,
He was shown into this room where Purity lay
And purchased false passion -
A passion for which he will forever pay -
An eternal debt
Collected and pocketed by Remorse and Regret
Who otherwise haunt him every hour of every day
With the sound of your beating heart.
You are the truth he ran from like a bullet from a gun;
You were an abandoned unborn son;
You were a baby with not even a manger

In the stable of the damned;
You were the baby caught by Lust's warm hands
And delivered into this crippled land
Where the outcasts work and the single mothers slave
To purchase the scraps at the sides of the plates
Of those who sweat with contentment
Of over-full stomachs,
Enjoying a quality of life that your mother
Could only dream of giving you.
You are a spirit from a whore's womb conceived,
The trade that invites Fornication's disease,
The trade that forces Death to come
Upon a mother who sells her body
For the good of her son.
You were an accidental arrow
Let loose in random flight
When the fingers of Nature's archer
Slipped in the night.
You were an error,
You were a mistake,
You, alone, are the Spirit of Hate.
You are Hate, without a mother,
You are Hate, who will never trust another.
You are Hate, and in this world that you blame
Sleep an army who have waited long for your name.
You are Hate, for whom millions will fight,
You are Hate, who gives war its right
To rise over Heaven's walls and above;
But know this -
You are Hate,
The bastard son of Fear after he gave up on Love.

CHAPTER VIII

**Hate's Prayer*

H: Gods, if you have ears, hear me now.
Save me.
Let my heart go numb,
Let my ears go deaf
And my voice keep mum.
Save me.
Let my skin go pale,
Don't fight the paralysis
From the sting of Truth's tail.
Save me.
Bury my name,
Let me disappear from the trail
And the hunters of Shame.
Save me.
Let my veins run cold,
Deaden the senses and nerves of my soul.
Save me.
Let me not feel,
Let me sell life's sensations,
I don't want what is real.

Hate turned and vanished into the night,
The Chosen Son, lost, out of sight.

Like a drifting nomad, he wandered for years,
Letting Time mask his face with age and beard;
Dead to the world did Hate disappear,
With only one name in his mind...
The Spirit of Fear.

CHAPTER IX

Far out along the wilderness to nowhere,
Where the winds barely blow
And the grasslands lay bare,
Where the river's given up
And the reeds pile up
In the stagnant backwater
(In which driftwood doesn't care
About never finding the sea),
Where daylight beats down on dry, arid dust
And burns and bakes the soil to a crust,
Where the heatwaves that hover softly above the ground
Make us believe there's something to be found
Just over the horizon,
Where the sun rises and sets for no other purpose
But to kill the hours of the day...
Here is where Hate found his way
To a dreamless town where Time doesn't go:
Where Solitude used to sit and watch grass fail to grow,
Where abandoned power plants, five leagues ahead,
Break the skyline of barren red sand
And cast long shadows over Desolation's desert land.
And in this town, where a rocking chair squeaks
And echoes through the idle street,
Where even the tumbleweed rests
And bakes in the heat,
Hate found a fellow, sitting, squinting at the sky.

CHAPTER IX

It had been years since Hate hadn't just passed someone by,
And such a long time in silence
Had made his voice older and dry;
But something in this fellow compelled him.
With his weather-worn face, rags attracting flies
And a slight nervous, jittering twitch in his eye,
Hate saw a fellow he thought he recognised.

H: *Do I know you?*
:   *Don't think so.*
H: *You seem familiar to me.*
:   *But how can we know that what we see*
       We have actually seen before?
       Memory and Imagination
       Oft pass through the same door
       And come back out in each other's clothes,
       And then which is which, who knows? Ha!
H: *I'm sure I've seen you before. What's your name?*
:   *Me? I'm Confusion.*
       Perhaps you met my half-brother, Illusion?
H: *He's your brother?*
Con: *Yes… At least I think so…*
       People say we've looked similar from the start
       And he occasionally drifts around these parts
       Though, most likely, you'll find him in the cities
       Dining with those who seek to impress,
       Who have bought into the notion that true success
       Is measured by the weight of our wealth,
       Where we are valued not in the choices we make
       But in the job we have and the salary we take
       That affords us the house in town,
       Driving the car with the rooftop down,

Filling our holes of dissatisfaction
With each new high-end contraption
We mistake for necessity.
Fine wares and fine foods,
Like the boy from nothing to the man made good,
He finally earns his office on the very top floor
Then looks out on the corporate skyline gore
And toasts to the system that has successfully
Pulled the wool over his eyes
And for years has sold him the beautiful lie
That the image is worth anything at all...
Yes, Illusion likes to drink with those yet to fall.

H: So how does one end up in a place like this?
Con: I could ask you the same question.
H: Well perhaps you've fallen from that fake floor of bliss.
Con: As perhaps have you.
H: I was never that high.
Con: Yet here we both are, under Disillusion's empty sky.

How strange, that we must first have a dream
To realise we are floating aimlessly downstream,
Going nowhere.
The plans we made, the aspirations we saved,
The loved ones we thought would hold us on rainy days
Are nothing but clouds and rainbows
Formed in wondrous shapes -
Postcard visions of the lives we hoped to make
That dissipate in the winds of Time,
Revealing paths to the unknown devoid of signs
To direct us in life.

H: I was never given the chance to dream.
Con: Or is that just how it seemed?
H: What's the point in dreaming

CHAPTER IX

       When you know full well you're awake?
       I don't rise in the morning for Fantasy's sake.
Con: *Ah, but you admit you chose your view?*
       After all, we are the choices we make.
H: *I am a product of choices made by others.*
Con: *Is that so? And is that the voice of one who suffers*
       Or just one schooled in the art of Blame,
       On unfounded theories from whence we came?
       But please, no! Sorry. Don't take offence.
       I'm just trying to see another side.
       It's a lifelong habit I struggle to hide.
       Call it 'the plague of a curious disposition' -
       One who endlessly finds themselves in the position
       Of standing in spirals of questions
       That seem to have no end.
H: *I knew him once.*
Con: *Who?*
H: *Curiosity. Though it seemed to me*
       Caution was his best friend.
Con: *Ah yes, now there's a confused mind,*
       Perhaps even more confused than mine,
       Bold and timid at the same time.
       He is fickle in his nature.
       He's a good soul yet I don't know why
       I used to give him the time of day.
       I think for him it might have been therapy
       But for me, his conversation was turmoil
       In an already sleepless brain,
       In a world where even Sanity
       Seemed to be going insane.
       But listen to me! Ha!
       I came here to stop asking questions

        Yet somehow I only find more;
        I'm stuck in silence with a mind I abhor
        For the things I can't understand;
        And so I spend the hours
        Just asking questions like I'm picking flowers,
        Examining some petals down to the finest symmetry
        While others I abandon with uncaring flippancy,
        Like man in his infancy.
        Oh, to see the whole world yet be blind to reality,
        The bliss of a child's eyes.

H: *What is reality?*
Con: *Ah, now there's the groove.*
H: *Is it no more than the painting of our own rationality?*
Con: *Goodness, now I'm confused.*
H: *At least you live up to your name.*
Con: *It's what we must do.*
H: *Unless we are Shame.*
Con: *Shame has his place,*
       As does Disgrace;
       They are the make-up artists for each other's face.
H: *That's quite an insight for Confusion's mind.*
Con: *I didn't say I was an idiot.*
       I said there are things I don't understand.
       The two things don't go hand in hand.
H: *What don't you understand?*
Con: *It would be quicker to publish what I know to be true,*
       For even simple knowledge like
       Blue is green and green is blue
       Seems up for debate.
       But, if you're asking what keeps me up at night,
       What glowing lamplights
       Do the moths of my mind precariously flutter around

CHAPTER IX

While trying not to get burned...
I suppose it's the mystery of living where our
Desire is concerned.
You can ask who we are,
But why do what we do?
Is it the wanting of our wants
That brings our colours out true?
I can understand wanting love and even pleasure
But then why do we destroy them in equal measure?
Why do we fight? Why do we kill?
Why does Greed clutch desperately to the will
Of our lives?
He has no currency in death.
And what's Pride's worth in his last dying breath?

H: *Pride is strong.*
Con: *Pride is wrong. Surely, he's missed the point.*
H: *Pride stands up for what he believes.*
Con: *No, that's Honour.*
And she is different in this air that we breathe.
I see Pride wield the sword of judgement
And I sometimes wonder if his own blood he'll spill.
H: *But if there is no life in death*
Then only in life can we fulfil
A sense of living.
Con: *And what is that fulfilment?*
And at what cost?
Is Illusion's dream worth it
If the next generation has lost
The teachings of Love and Compassion?
H: *The illusion is that those teachings*
Exist in any more than a fashion
Affordable to those of the privileged and rich,

Whose indulgences react in a recurring itch
That's soothed with philanthropic treatments
When the rash on the conscience is too much to bear;
And with that same wealth
Can you buy back your honour
After your sins so foul and unfair.
If ever I kill, I will have Hypocrisy
Represent me in the Court of Law,
For <u>there</u> is the practitioner
Who works with the flaw
That we are all self-serving,
And that saint-veiled judges are no more deserving
Of the keys to liberty
As they sit there preserving their own sense of dignity.
Open your eyes and see the world for what it is.

Con: *I have learned not to trust my eyes*
To find clear sight,
For they are so often blinded
By things that shine bright
Or even just misguided
By the fractures in the light.
We must look to our hearts to find
Our way through the unknown.

H: *Yet one's moral compass is so easily thrown*
Off course by the magnetic power of our will to survive.

Con: *No, it's thrown off course by the teachings of Fear:*
That to live in love is no more than a lie!

Suddenly Hate's tongue froze...
Like a hawk to its prey his vision zoned in close.
"What do you know of Fear?" Hate asked.
Confusion shivered in the sudden change in the air.

CHAPTER IX

"Not much," he replied. *"Only that he lives here."*
As if Desire and Purpose had long been asleep,
Something stirred within Hate, buried deep.
He lifted his gaze and looked around;
Confusion's words were like blood to the hound.

H: *Where does he reside?*
Con: *Eh...he has no fixed abode,*
      Often in the bar, and then on the roadside.
      You will identify him as a shadow of life,
      Eroded by the torrents and gales of Regret.
      I can't speak of his history for I have never asked
      But he seems like a soul so tormented by his past
      That he would sooner choose to repent
      By choking out his life with the hands of Contempt
      If he wasn't so afraid of the road that connects
      The end of this life and the beginning of the next.
      I suppose his religion is the same
      As all the others at play:
      The unknowns of death are what lead us to pray
      And obey the Gods' laws, hoping we'll be saved.
      But what business have you with Fear?
H: *He owes a debt of justice to one held dear.*
      I'm glad we met.

And off Hate set, down the road,
Confusion watching him turn and go,
The dust kicking up behind his feet;
Then around the corner
He vanished from the street.

CHAPTER X

The heat of the day mercilessly beat down
On the last of the living in this barren wee town.
While the rattlesnake hid in the tumbleweed's shade,
The scorpion burrowed deep to escape the searing heatwave
Of the midday sun.
But Hate welcomed the elements and welcomed the burn
As his eyes scanned through the swirls of sand
And the glints of cactus needles -
The daytime stars shimmering on the land.
The winds hushed.
The dust settled.
In the distance appeared an old worn shack
With saloon doors obscuring a room almost
Black in shadow.
Hate's field of vision narrowed.
With each step closer to the old saloon doors
A violent mood ignited his core,
Pulsing, growing, glowing -
Then suddenly...
It tempered at the sound
Of an incomprehensible, warbling refrain
Being mumbled nearby in drunken strain.
He followed the tune round the side of the inn...
And there before him...
A wasted drunk, with a beer and a gin,
Almost asleep on his feet, his forehead against the wall,

CHAPTER X

Staring at his dignity, letting the splashing piss fall
And bounce back onto his legs.
Hate's heart arrested
By a feeling in his soul aching to be contested.
Was this he?
The coward who abandoned a mother-to-be,
The father never there for a child to see,
Was this he?
Fitting Confusion's description almost perfectly,
The unanswered question answered at last,
The missing link in the chain of Hate's past,
Was this he?
Could it be?
The pillar of support a mum never had,
Life's absent good times when times got bad?
It couldn't be.
Hate looked on, trying to settle the questions in his head,
Then finally said,
"You're pissing on your shoes."
"It's not the dick's fault, it's the feet that need to move,"
Came the slurring reply.

H: *You're having a good day, it seems to be?*
Drunk: *Just another day in the land of the free.*
H: *Free from what?*
Dr: *Whatever chains you've got*
       Around your hands and feet,
       And the judges your sobriety just can't defeat.

And with a smile both sincere and wry
The drunk then clumsily pulled up his fly,
And on his tattered trousers rubbed his hands dry

Before observing the stranger through his better eye.

Dr: So what brings you here?
        Or like most of us, is it just the price of the beer?
H: I'm searching for something.
Dr: Aren't we all? Or perhaps you're running?
        There is always writing on the wall.
H: If only we knew what it said.
Dr: If you knew where to find it would you have it read?
        There is freedom in ignorance.
        How often do we choose to remain unaware
        And preoccupy ourselves with the
        Whats, whys and wheres
        Of the crosswords and puzzles of Irrelevance?
H: Or just by getting drunk.
Dr: Perhaps the best way to be.
H: Living outside of reality?
Dr: Of yours, perhaps, and of your mentality;
        For who, while we live, is truly qualified
        To define real life?
        The beggar lives in a different world to the king
        Yet they share the same air;
        While one believes in the divine right of his living,
        The other curses a world unfair.
        Don't judge another for trying to see life
        In different colours. We all have our demons.
        ...It's strange, I swear I've never seen your face
        Yet you feel like a memory I can't quite place.
        Have we met before?

"Memory and Imagination oft pass through the same door,"
Hate calmly said,

CHAPTER X

Using Confusion's teachings to keep his cards unread.
"*So true,*" came the reply,
Trying to focus through inebriated eyes.

Dr: *So, what are you searching for?*
       Or is it some<u>one</u>?
       How often the heart has us chasing the sun
       For what feels like a lifetime,
       Searching for the soul who can offer eternal sunshine.
H: *It's rare to find such a soul.*
       Most settle for square pegs in round holes
       Forced in as best they can.
       Leave it there long enough
       And the peg eventually sticks and jams
       With the rust and dust of the relationship;
       Two spirits forever interlocked,
       Not for the values for which Friendship fought
       But because they are stuck in familiar grooves
       Which deepen as they rot.
Dr: *You have either observed well the life of your elders*
       Or Nature has been kind and given you shelter
       From the harsh weather of Age and Time,
       For such an insight isn't learned
       In the count of your years but in mine.

"How old are you?" the drunk asked with his drunken smile.
"Old enough to see through the writings
That gave Love her name,
And the naive teachings that shot her to fame," Hate replied.
At that moment, the swaying drunkard found his balance,
As if a shot of sobriety had gone straight to his head;
All of the voices inside went silent

At the hearing of the name that had just been said.
Then, trying to hold his voice steady, the drunk remarked,
"Many would argue those teachings have kept millions alive."
"And yet some would argue that to live in love
Is no more than a lie... No?"
Hate watched carefully
For the faintest flicker in the drunk's eye.
"That the teachings have done nothing
But impaired our strength to survive;
To live protected within Love's sanctuary I'm sure is great,
But what of those stranded outside the gate?"
Hate continued,
Wondering if he could stretch the sinews
Of the drinker's drunken countenance
And split the smiling mask.

H: *But I'm sure Love's fine.*
       Her best-sellers made her a celebrity
       For your generation and mine;
       And in the Gods' hall of fame
       Will she no doubt be enshrined,
       While her teachings get regurgitated
       Until the end of time.

Hate watched the drunk look to the ground
As if, in the dirt, may some peace be found
From the memories of ghosts and the ghosts of memories
That had somehow awakened in the cemetery of his past
And were rising up through the overgrown grass.
Then, coming back to the stare of Hate,
He lifted his chest, held himself straight,
And letting boastful bubbles surface like booze

CHAPTER X

To display an honourable froth, said,

> **I Knew Love Once,*
> *Back In A Happier Day*

Dr: It may not seem likely to look at me now but...

    I knew Love once, back in a happier day,
    When Youth cared not for tomorrow,
    Back when we were just children at play
    In a world innocent of sorrow.

    She gave me her heart and I gave her mine
    And we cured our desire's ill health;
    As penniless paupers, in the poorest of times,
    We would steal the joys of Heaven itself.

    She made you feel like your flaws were freckles
    Of beauty that came out in the sun;
    In a world where we're nothing
    But the black sheet's smallest speckle,
    She made you feel like someone.

    Her own fair beauty was so faint to the eye
    That even Vanity could not detect;
    Her kindness and grace could make Pride cry
    For off Love's soul does your own love reflect.

    Jealousy's words to Love's patient ears
    Were like pins into a cushion;
    Under the skin would pricks of pain disappear
    And turn pointless within Love's constitution.

To want to live, not to be loved,
But to share the world with another,
If such feeling lies in Heaven above
Love is surely the angels' mother.

But when Love loves you more than life itself,
As loyal as the tide to the sea,
How is one worthy of life's purest wealth?
There's so much I could never give or be.

What do we do when the armour we wear
Inevitably slips from our chest,
And our faults and failings are left naked and bare,
Exposing their hero as a willing fool at best?

We grab at lies like children to sweets
To protect our self-made facade;
Can we never admit we're scared of defeat
When Uncertainty tries to drive the mind mad?

Yet, how do we know if we are on the right path:
If the flame of this match will forever glow -
And light our way to the end,
Where we still dance and laugh -
Or will it burn out...
And in darkness we know not where to go?

But Love was never scared of the unknown,
Even when Youth grew older;
Even when Romance's fashions we'd outgrown,
Love remained in the heart of its beholder.

But my heart, for Future's fates did it search,
Letting present joys blow away in the gales;
On the top of my ship did the black crow perch
As into the seas of Doubt I set sail.

How worthless the soul that is barren of self-belief.
Being loved by others will never be strength enough.
The giving of love is how we heal wounds of Grief,
But first, one must learn to show love to self-worth.

And so I fled, with my feeble heart,
Knowing not who or what I should be.
Taking with me mistakes and regrets on my part
I hoped somehow I would set Love free.

I knew Love once, back in a happier day,
When Youth cared not for tomorrow;
But how cruel is life, to recall that child at play
And yet, feel nothing but sorrow.

Hate watched a tear run down the drunk's cheek
As he came to the end of his heartfelt speech,
Conducted, seemingly, by the ghost of Contrition.
But not even the sounds of a sorrowful cello
Could soften Hate's condition:
Feelings of rage and violence were
Forging in his fiery furnaces deep within.
This had to be he,
The figure he had waited so many years to see.
But what does one do when the servant of Injustice,
Who tore your life in two,
Now stands as helpless as the victim,

As if long abandoned by the leader who picked him?
With the fire of Conviction being stoked with every thought,
Hate took in the image of the one he believed Destiny
Had brought him to find:
This twisted hypocrite of nature
Who stands up for Love in song and voice,
Yet turned his back on the destitute when he had the choice.
But, even now, something was holding a rash temper at bay,
As if the compassion of his mother somewhere lay
Woven within the finest threads of his DNA
That lined the core of his being,
Like the part of man that strives to keep believing
In humanity in the face of injustice.
With confusion and doubt fighting just below the surface,
Hate steadied his breath
And put the drunk's fate to one final test.

H: *And is there anyone else for whose name*
         You would offer the tears of Regret and Shame?
Dr: *...Only for Love can I shed such a tear.*

Hate's eyes filled with hatred clear.
The world fell silent and all it could hear
Was the death of Hate's mercy as it singed and seared
On his scorching reply:
"I couldn't expect any more from the Spirit of Fear, Could I?"
The drunk froze...
Paleness began to grow on his face
As his name's true colours appeared.

F: *Who are you? Who are you, to whom the etiquette*
       Of introductions clearly doesn't adhere?

CHAPTER X

*You Are He

H: *I am your writing on the wall,*
The spirit that will hear your scream as you fall
Down into the depths of Hell,
For you are he:

The coward who abandoned a mother-to-be,
The father never there for a child to see,
The reason I was born onto the stage of Misery
And forced into the chorus of Plight and Poverty.
You are he:
The unanswered question answered at last,
The missing link in the chain of my past,
The one that fled the scene so fast
Remorse failed to take him in her grasp.
You are he:
The pillar of support a mum never had,
Life's absent good times when times got bad,
He who robbed a child of a dad
And all the joy a dad could add.
You are he,
Who was never at my side
To see me succeed and cheer with pride.
In those teenage years, in those vulnerable tides,
Where were you that should have been my guide?
You are he,
Who was never there
For all those moments a family should share,
Who left us forever one short of a prayer
And exposed in the open to the arrows of Despair.
Are you not he,

Who traded faithfulness for base infidelity?
Who fucked a teenager, raping their destiny -
A crime for which my mother paid the penalty!
You are he,
Whom I vow never to be.
You are the coward who abandoned
A mother-in-need,
Whom from Destitution's chains
Would never be freed
While the wounds of her past
Would forever bleed;
I only hope that now she sleeps in peace.
But you, who sowed your fatal seed
The day you ran,
Your weak, worthless soul
Is at the mercy of the damned.
You ask, "Who am I?"
I am Hate:
Your mistake that forever sealed your fate.

Fear's breath stopped,
Stuck in time like the second hand of the clock
That desperately spasms between its tick and its tock.

H: Tell me, how does it feel
    To have the end of your life become so real?
    What can you see?
F: I imagine it's the figure of my mortality.
H: So here we are at last, drunk or sober
    Yet seeing the same reality.

"I beg you, please!" Fear gasped, crumbling to his knees.

CHAPTER X

H: And where were you at Purity's pleas?
        I am the bastard son of Purity
        And now you will feel the purity of pain
        As the teeth of Hell's rats gnaw through your veins
        And feed on your heart as your cold blood drains.
F: From a father to his son, I beg let Forgiveness come
        For all I am to blame.
H: I would rather spend a hundred years wed to Shame
        Than admit having you as my family name.

And with that, Hate pulled out a gun.
Fear stood paralyzed in fright,
Like a rabbit stunned in a freight train's headlights.

H: Your reputation precedes you
        And it's clear to see the world doesn't need you.
F: No, please don't send me to Death,
        I fear I will hang -

BANG!

Fear. Dead.
His last words cut short by a single piece of lead.
His last vision of this world, the barrel of a gun,
Before the trigger was pulled by his one true son.
Hate breathed a sigh of relief
While inside his soul, something unleashed.
There he stood, a desire fulfilled;
There he stood, a spirit who had killed.
There he stood, one released from the power of Fear,
The power he believed holds us back from the frontier
Of our true potential.

In the death of Fear he felt immune to Remorse;
In the death of Fear had he altered his course.
In that act, he had opened the gate
And let his heart fill with blood of pure hate.
"*Spirits,*" he said,

*Hate's Call To The Downtrodden

H: Spirits, hear me. Hear me;
All of you who lived by Fear, hear me.
All of you who followed the sermons of Doubt,
Come out. Come out;
Come out from that house of prayer -
There is nothing left for you there,
Come out. Come out;
Come out, walk away from your faith,
Let your god lay to waste
And follow me. Follow me;
Follow me and I will set you free.
I have come, for all that's been done,
I have come, your one true son.
I guarantee I will give you purpose;
All of you who wish to be more than surplus
On this land, take my hand.
Take my hand and follow me. Follow me.
Follow me and I will set you free.
I have come, for all that's been done,
I have come, your one True Son!
Rage, I will teach you to never subside
And you will march up front at the side of Pride.
Pride, hear me! Come and you will see,
I will show you how great and how strong you can be.

CHAPTER X

Guilt! I will show you it's not your fault -
Follow me and let us make an assault
On all those who walk and march with Grace
But do nothing;
Those who leave the poor as their own poor race,
Hoping they will never rise from their place.
Spirits, follow me, follow me!
Follow me and I will set you free.
Anointed, famed, appointed, proclaimed,
I am he!
I am he that has come.
I am The One.
I am The One, The Chosen Son!
Rise. Rise!
Rise above the pitch of your screams
And your cries
That you've been told no one can hear;
You were told that by Fear,
And now Fear is dead!
Feel your new-found strength.
Follow Hate, and let this new gospel spread.

CHAPTER XI

Can you hear that? Boom boom boom
Can you hear that? Boom boom boom
Can you hear that? Boom boom boom
It's the rat-a-tat-tat and tat of the drums
Can you hear that? Boom boom boom
Can you hear that? Boom boom boom
Can you hear that? Boom boom boom
It's the rat-at-tat-tat of all that comes
Can you hear that? Boom boom boom
Can you hear that? Boom boom boom
Can you hear that? Boom boom boom
It's the rat-a-tat-tat and bat of the drums
Can you hear that? Boom boom boom
Can you hear that? Boom boom boom
Can you hear that? Boom boom boom
It's the rat-a-tat of all that comes
As the drums of war begin to beat
And in perfect time comes the marching of feet.

Hate marched from bay to bay
Collecting every waif and stray,
The orphans of Fortune with nothing to say
Until now.
But how loud grows the voice of a united crowd,
Unified with Revenge, courageous and proud -
Proud to die

CHAPTER XI

In a war to wake all sleeping dogs
That lie.
They marched o'er the plains;
They marched through the towns,
Knocking on the doors of tin shacks run down.
They marched o'er highways,
Down into the trench,
And collected those scented with Mortality's stench.
They marched through villages
Forgotten by the state
Who found their new leader in words of Hate.
Then they marched to the harbours
And queued at the quay
And the ships of Revolt were set out to sea.
And towards the capital
And provinces elite
They sailed and marched, dying to greet
Idleness and Leisure,
Who were drinking with Pleasure,
Chinking to Prosperity in full double measures -
The leaders of the world toasting Success,
Deaf to the needing and Suffering's requests.
But while Illusion sat there
Watching it all,
He soon noticed the rumbling pictures on the wall -
He felt the vibrations
Under his feet
Of the rhythms, chants, marches and beats
Of the drums and sounds
Of Revolution's ring,
And knew who was coming and the terror they'd bring.
They had nothing to live for,

Nothing to lose,
And knew that the leaders didn't have a clue.
But it was all too late -
Then came the SMASH
Of a brick coming through the ornate stained glass.
Legions scaled walls,
Piled into the rooms,
While cigar smoke made rings of impending doom.
The leaders all scattered,
Then fell to their knees
As bullets riddled the ceiling with ease.
Their time was up;
It was time to pay,
It was time for the outcasts to have their say.
So they lined the halls
With leaders and all,
And asked them who wished to be the first to fall.
And for pardon they pleaded
And begged for their lives
But were told only the courts of Hell could decide.
"For that's what you gave us
So that's all we know,
It was you that told us, 'You reap what you sow.'"
The rattle of shots
Rang into the air
And then rose the cheer of those neglected of care;
Those shunned by Courtesy,
Ignored by Recognition,
They were the living painting of society's condition.
And then, through the streets,
The mob united
And, rallied by Rage, celebration ignited!

CHAPTER XI

Belongings piled high,
The bonfire lit,
The night air ablaze with raging flames fit
For the God of Fury
Craving sacrifice -
But when does it stop? How many pay the price?

"How many watched," Hate yelled,

H: *In silent reflection*
With no more than head shakes of passive objection?
Where is Innocence?
His head's on the line;
A clean-handed bystander is as much a crime
As murder committed
By selfish disregard.
How many are to blame for Suffering's scars?
How many did nothing
But offer a prayer
To water a conscience barren of care?
How many hoped
That somebody else
Would carry the torch as they watched from the shelf?
How many slept
While Misfortune thrived?
All are complicit who close their eyes
At Misery's dawn
And Affliction's hot noon;
Well, now you'll see Violence by the light of the moon.
The Gods will watch as we build our new kingdom
On the ruins of Heaven's promises,
And on the rubble of Love!

And SpiritLand quaked,
Trembled down to its core,
The roads split: Hell had opened its door.
Out came the damned,
The forgotten, the neglected,
As brothers in arms in this vengeful collective;
Buses were tipped,
Cars were crashed,
Exhausts set alight, and the heat from the blasts
Torched the parks,
Scorched the trees,
And flames ran wild - wild and free.
And with clouds of ash
The night air choked
And eyes streamed blood from the sting of the smoke.
Bottles were tossed,
Children threw rocks,
While objects were flung out of high-rise tower blocks:
Sound systems, beds,
Ovens! Settees!
The news of the world, no longer on TV
But finally come,
Finally here;
It's finally live, playing out loud and clear!
You can't turn it off,
No channels to change -
Welcome to reality and the truth of its pain!
And while Chaos ran rampant
In the old town square,
Each frightened soul fled their own frightened nightmare;
Some ran this way,
Others bolted that,

CHAPTER XI

The bell tower clanged and they all scattered like bats.
But through the cold darkness
One pair of legs
Ran for dear life through the city's dank dregs;
Running in panic,
Running in fright,
It was Reason running through this mad, senseless night.
He was trying to escape
The gang chasing behind -
The rabble of terror in lawless design,
Growling their curses,
Barking abuse,
Chasing new blood like rabid hounds set loose.
Such a gentle, soft soul
Of caution and thought,
Not fit for a world where Thought's left to rot;
Only a miracle
Could keep him alive
And miracles are scarce where Hopelessness thrives.
But still he ran on,
Cutting through wynds,
Not daring to look back at what was behind.
He dipped round a corner,
Out of sight -
CRACK!
A hook to the throat came in from the right.
Reason went down,
Flat on his back,
Winded and choking as the mob in pack
Clawed and mauled
And howled their cheers
That drowned out the screams only Reason could hear

As they tore at his shirt,
And wrenched at his limbs,
And smashed in his kneecaps and battered his shins;
As they snapped all his fingers,
And stamped through his teeth,
And kicked in his head as it bled on the concrete.
Then they all took turns
To swing at his ribs
And take gleeful delight in the sound it would give:
The whack of the bat,
The thud of the cane,
The pummelling of fists as they thrived on the pain!
They chewed off his ear,
They plied at his teeth,
Then held his eyes open to blind them with bleach.
And Reason wailed
Gut curdling cries,
Then the ground fell beneath him and he started to rise;
On a sea of arms
He was paraded and tossed
As they proceeded towards their makeshift cross.
They nailed up his hands,
They nailed up his feet,
And the portrait of pain was almost complete.
They stoned him for fun,
They lashed him for laughs,
Until Reason's pleas faded weak and fast...
Then the crowds dispersed,
Bored of their game,
And went hunting for another to do exactly the same.
They left him to die
On a cross on the wall;

CHAPTER XI

Reason, crucified
For no reason at all.

The Death Of Reason

And in the death of Reason, the world's scales collapsed;
In chaotic imbalance, Sanity lost all grasp -
"In the name of Justice" was a thing of the past.
In the death of Reason, killers craved their next kill,
But when hit after hit began to deaden the thrill,
To heighten the senses, more blood was spilled.
In the death of Reason, Madness and Insanity
Began to believe they held the power of the galaxy
And put weapons of terror into the hands of Depravity.
And in the death of Reason, Logic and Sense
Were put on trial for treason with lies and pretence.
They were executed at dawn
And guiltless lives the world over suffered the consequence
As pointless Rage raged on;
For when Rage loves Rage,
Their children are self-made,
And their futile cause infects each new age.

CHAPTER XII

And so, in the relentless scarring of Time,
The world turned black and blue
As War limped on, beaten and bruised,
Through his own no-man's land.
Innocence lay there, facedown in the dirt,
Next to Happiness, impaled, crimson red
Soaking through the family photo in his shirt.
His frightened eyes drew over to Courage,
Who had fallen again and again,
And again and again,
Before being gunned down by Survival
Who proved stronger in the end.
Bravery hung motionless on the rusting barbed wire
While, further off, Youth
Lay drowned in the mire.
Optimism had died with a smile on his face;
And while his top half rested here,
His legs had landed in some other place.
Temperance, Beauty, Wisdom, Grace,
And countless others laid to waste,
Nothing more than meat for the flies
Feasting on a landfill of bodies piled high.

And in the heat of the afternoon sun
On one war-worn day,
Hate appeared in a field of blood

And found Death, an exhausted slave,
Harvesting corpses from the dried-up mud.

H: *I promised you, Death, and it's come to fruition.*
       In this life, only the dead are forgiven.

The guardian of the afterlife looked on,
Sweat on his brow,

D: *When does it end?*
       Is there a limit to hatred?
       Or is there nothing in this world
       That is worth keeping sacred?

Hate looked Death straight in the eye
And, in steel-hardened resolve,
Gave his reply:

H: *When Love, Kindness and Compassion die,*
       And the world is rid of their self-righteous lie,
       Then, Death, you may rest.
       Tell me where they hide
       For I can feel they still breathe.
D: *They are nothing more than poor refugees.*
       Just let them be.
H: *Let them be? Let them be?!*
       Those who shut their eyes and ears to me
       And so many others, who put faith in them
       Like we do in our mothers?
       Where is Love? Where is Kindness?
       We preach them like prophets
       Then hope they don't find us

When we walk past Despair holding his coinless cup.
The promise of Love is as fickle as Fear;
Yet, in Love are we told that Salvation is near.
How many have died waiting for her to appear?
How many relied on Compassion to survive
And believed, in their life, that Kindness would thrive,
Only to learn that the soil of their slums
Has too long been deprived
Of the water of good-will to let moral fibre flourish,
Township after township completely malnourished
Of hope and trust,
Condemned to a future worth less than the dust
On their feet.
Let them be? No. Let's bury the cliché
That Love will set us free.
Perhaps then we would have the courage
To shake off our attire
Of the saints of Grace to which we aspire,
And expose our true selves as the sinners and liars
That we are.
At least then we would know how far
We have strayed from the stars of Redemption
And wouldn't risk being betrayed by Hope's deception.

"Don't you dare mention his name!" Death bit back,
"He was a saviour who didn't deserve to fall."
"Hope?" Hate snapped,

H: Hope was the Devil's most cunning creation of all.
       Hope was the bastard that wouldn't let Despair die.
       Hope was the prison-guard keeping
       The downtrodden in place

CHAPTER XII

     While they ignorantly served the wealthier race,
     Being sold the myth that Happiness and Freedom
     Sat just around the corner, open-armed.
     In robes and sandals he walked among us disguised,
     His whole life pulling the wool over our eyes
     And even the eyes of Truth.

D: *And where is your proof?*

H: *This world's poverty is my proof -*
     My youth is my proof -
     I don't need to hear it from Truth.

D: *Just as well, for I watched him lose his life*
     On the hangman's noose,
     Tried in a court of fools
     On a book blank of constitution and rule;
     Corruption at the helm of the entire prosecution
     While a jury of jesters sought their own retribution;
     Revenge at the bench, leading the session,
     Having already written the false confession.
     We live in a world where Greed has been throned
     In the high courts of Justice,
     Where all he had to do to abolish Morality's decree
     Was rip the eyes from his soul
     So his conscience couldn't see.
     You may have killed Truth,
     But at least we still have Honesty.

H: *Ah yes, haha! Truth's protégé,*
     Whose words fall deaf on anyone
     Concerned with self-preservation.
     The principled politician who will never see office
     For, despite the preachings he prays will fall upon us,
     The manifestos of Reputation and Pride
     Are what resonate in our hearts,

Where honest desires reside -
The selfish flaws of our being we try so hard to hide.
Don't put your faith in Honesty, Death!
He is a naive fool absolving his sins
In a pharisee's box of confession,
In a building where charlatans perfect their profession.
Don't make me the object of your hateful obsession;
We hold each other in higher regard...
I'll let you get on,
For your workload here is clear to see
And we both have business and places to be.
But, before I go...
For all that I may slate the nature of Honesty,
Please take my parting words
With the honesty of Nature:
Of all the spirits I have ever known,
My faith is pure only for you;
In these fickle winds,
From which even the steadfast birds have flown,
Still you keep your word, straight and true.
When the shadows fall over my final few breaths,
My respect for you will remain undying.
If only, in this world, love was as certain as death...
Perhaps we might not crawl into it crying.

Death watched Hate turn and leave,
Stepping through life's decaying remains
As if they were fallen autumn leaves
Waiting to be taken back into the earth.
Then he threw back his reply,
For what it was worth.

CHAPTER XII

D: *Someday you will want to leave this world, Hate,*
     And I won't come to get you.
     And you will live for eternity
     In this purgatory you have made;
     For in a world without Forgiveness
     There will be no one here to save you.

Hate heard...but didn't turn back.

CHAPTER XIII

Under crumbling bridges and over empty highways,
Along concrete ridges and through forgotten byways
Hate walked on, through nation and nation,
Each one a work of Terror and Devastation.
He was a small dot walking through
The landscape of Dereliction,
A landscape fit for Destruction's depiction
Of his perfect world.
As if, in the gallery of the Gods, their most priceless painting,
Our living planet, in all the colours of its creating,
Had been scored and scraped,
While the oil paint clung desperately to the canvas in flakes.
Underneath, the artist's pencilled sketches showed through
In a mess of greys and fading pale hues -
A work of beauty, so old and rare,
Defaced and sabotaged beyond repair.
This was the world through which Hate walked;
And through the ash-thickened breeze and shattered rock,
Everywhere was soundscaped by the soft drop of bombs
Massaging the ground with pummels of doom,
Rumbling gently,
Like the muffled bass vibrating in the next room.

And just as the weeks and months
Were paling into insignificance,
It was then, in the desert, far off in the distance,

CHAPTER XIII

That Hate heard sounds of life carrying over on the wind.
As he approached a border into a foreign land,
Where makeshift tents battled storms of sands
That whipped through the wreckage
Of a once quaint, peaceful dwelling,
Hate found the source of faint echoes and swellings;
A pig-squeal like din
Retching from the souls of poor orphaned children,
Wailing over the burnt flesh and bones of loved ones:
Begging not to be forgotten by Death,
Begging for an end to Life's senseless quest,
Begging to be reunited with their mums and dads
Than suffer living hell in the world of the mad.
But Mercy was long dead, slain by Retribution's knife,
And Suicide had escaped, taking his own life.

And while Hate walked through
These living tableaux shaped by Grief,
He came across a familiar face
Sitting on the ground, staring into space,
His knees clutched into his chest
As he rocked back and forth in a catatonic arrest
Of shock...
It was Confusion, lost way beyond the realms of his thought,
Locked in a cycle of a single word as he rocked...
"Why...? Why...? Why...?"
"Confusion,"
Hate said, waiting for a reply.
"Why...? Why...? Why...?" The mad patient repeated,
Long abandoned by the asylum where the insane are treated.
Hate crouched down and looked deep into his eyes,
Wondering where he had gone.

"Why...? Why...? Why...?" Confusion went on.
"Why what?" Hate said.
"Why...?" came the reply, looking straight past Hate's head.
"Confusion. It's me. Hate."
But Confusion looked right through him,
In his lost, confused state.
Hate slapped his face and gave his shoulders a shake,
"Confusion, come back to me. Come back for god's sake."
But it was too late.
Confusion was so far beyond the boundaries of his mind
He had abandoned his body as a living shell locked in time.
So desperate to flee the horrors and senseless crimes of war,
He had locked the door back to his sanity
And thrown away the keys.
This was the price for a sense of inner peace
In a world of hate.
Confusion's inner being was free from this reality
In all but one word that didn't escape:
"Why...? Why...? Why...?"

Hate turned around to see
What Confusion's view would forever be
In his frozen, shell-shocked form;
He noticed his gaze was set upon a soft light
Glowing through the haze, far off, just above the horizon,
Like a lighthouse, stranded, naked on desert sand,
As the ocean, drained of water, reveals its barren land.
And he had no sooner taken in the soft light
When something else came into his sight -
A canvas tent with its doors flapping from side to side
While, inside, shadows did their best to hide.
"Once again," Hate said,

CHAPTER XIII

Looking down at Confusion's empty head,
"I'm glad we met. Once again you have led me
To where my desire is set."
Violent winds forced the sun's descent
As Hate drew near to the battered tent.
With his gun at his side, composed in hand,
A choir of angels, in crescendo, sang
Their most haunting hymn,
Conducted by Revenge, composed by Sin;
Hate felt his heart burn within
As he pushed open the canvas to reveal...
A band of exiles, cramped, head to heel,
Cowered on the floor,
Blood-stained, mud-stained, with nothing to live for
But the lives of each other.
And propped up with bags at the side,
Under the drooping canvas,
An old, exhausted soul was being nursed.
Her head was being held up
As a child poured the last remains of soup into her mouth
From a dish, cracked and chipped,
While a stabbing pain attacked her
As she swallowed every sip.
It was Kindness, being held by those she'd managed to save,
Clinging to the notion of seeing another day.
Sharp, sheering shrapnel from a random, thoughtless mine
Had sliced through her stomach to the nerves of her spine,
Leaving her paralyzed down from the waist,
While able arms did their best to keep her organs in place.
Kindness was fading,
Being kept alive by the last survivors
Who believed she was worth saving -

A union made up of all creeds and colours,
A band of strangers turned sisters and brothers
And mothered by Compassion,
Who stood right there, between her children and intruder,
In the rarest of fashions -
The fashion of quiet, unjudging respect for life
In all of its forms.
From the largest of lions to the weakest lamb born,
From the strongest of men to the child deformed,
She only ever saw Nature's design
And lived in the belief that compassion offered
Would return in kind.
Hate stood there disarmed by her apparent lack of fear,
As if she was a warrior who had thrown down her spear
And then continued to lower her shield,
With an honest countenance that says no knife is concealed.
Exposed yet composed, Compassion stood steadfast
And took Hate in with her soft, caring eyes
That sent his mind flying back into his past;
As if Time's bent and broken hands had rewound
And, somewhere in space, Chance had found
The one thing in life Hate missed the most -
In that moment, Hate saw his mother in ghost.
The purity of Compassion
Reflected at him the compassion of Purity -
The love for a son that remains in perpetuity.
But even in these deceptions created by Time,
Hate would not be fooled.
As he regripped his gun, Sorrow was overruled by Rage
As the author of the next unwritten page of Hate's tale.
"The sands of your time have run," he said.
"Bullets of false revenge are what lay poised

In the chamber of that gun,"
Compassion answered, in a gentle voice.

Com: *And never forget that we always have a choice*
          No matter how bleak the day.
H: *So did everyone else who ever chose to turn away.*
          And so here we are;
          If compassion was foolproof we would not need
          The scars to remind us
          Of all the times we were betrayed by Kindness,
          Who now lies here, a victim of her own hypocrisy.
Com: *She lies here a victim of Hate's autocracy,*
          After the sounds of bomb shells drowned out her voice.
H: *What drowned out Penury's voice?*
          The passive footsteps of Apathy?
          The chitter-chatter of those who happily
          Turn the other cheek, while pretending
          They are disciples of the practice you preach?
          The tramp that has a voice to ask for Kindness
          Receives nothing more than society's blindness.
          And if he so wishes to come back into sight,
          He must first endure Poverty's plight,
          Being battered in the night by the bats and canes
          Of Deprivation's delight,
          By Starvation, Disease, and Winter's bite.
          And once Horror and Pain have sculpted their image
          Of such unavoidable fright,
          Then, and only then, will the tramp
          Have his moment in the spotlight,
          While waiting in desperation
          For the darkness of Death.
          This was the world of so-called Compassion

    That I witnessed. Don't talk to me about choice
    For you have never been there in body or voice.
Com: *We were always there Hate, your whole life;*
    Kindness and Grace were trying to guide
    But the office of Greed will always seek to divide
    The will of the many for the wealth of the few.
    He profits when he pits me against you.
    I am here, but to recognise compassion
    We must first drop the guard from our hearts
    And let ourselves be loved.
    To walk through your life in fear and distrust
    Is to only ever see a world unjust;
    And when Hope appears in his humble, true name,
    Do not be blinded by misplaced blame
    Nor fooled by Corruption and Illusion's game
    That we may take the role of the Gods.
    No one has, and will never have
    The right to take another's life.

"Yet we have given ourselves the right to ignore it,"
Hate said, as cold as ice.
So callous, so cold,
Compassion could feel a sharp pang in her soul
As she feared Hate was too far lost to be saved;
In a prison of his hatred, he was his self-made slave.
In darkening resolve, Hate lifted his gun,
Pressed it up against Compassion's breast
And took in the face of the one
He had dreamed for so long of laying to rest.

H: *The least you can do is fight for your life*
    For only fools believe in a martyr's paradise.

CHAPTER XIII

**Compassion's Last Request*

Com: Cut off my hands
           And I will be handless,
           Still, I will embrace you with my arms.
           Tear off my arms
           And I will be armless,
           Still, I will embrace you with my words.
           Rip out my tongue
           And I will be speechless,
           Yet, still, I will embrace you with my eyes.
           Pull out my eyes
           And I will be blind,
           Still, I will embrace you with my heart.
           Tear out my heart?
           I will be heartless.
           And so, let me die, for I am of no good to this world.

Silence...

Bang.

Faster than words we didn't mean to say,
In an instant, lifeless, at Hate's feet Compassion lay
As her blood soaked the sand red.
But Hate, expecting to be flooded with elation great,
Instead looked upon her motionless,
As if this act of revenge was somehow tokenless.
He felt empty, cold,
His well of sensation left hollow and holed,
Drained away.
Taking in the eyes of his audience, he then found Kindness,

Who looked back at him, accepting her fate,
Which sat ready in waiting
In the form of his weapon's final round.
But instead, in vacant gaze and mute to sound,
He let the smoking gun drop to the ground.
He turned,
Drifted out of the tent and sight,
And disappeared into the haze of the cool desert night.

*"Are we but shooting stars in the night
Or is our course mapped out in the sky?
In death will I learn the meaning of life
Or learn it was all a meaningless lie?
Was it all pre-made, this part I played,
Or did I choose my own evens and odds?
Or were my joys and pain
No more than chips in a game
Of roulette between Fate and the Gods?"*

CHAPTER XIV

As aimless and lost as a paper bag in the wind,
Hate wandered through the black, cold, sandy expanse,
Lost in a trance for nights and days on end.
And whether consciously or not,
He was making his way towards that soft, golden haze
That Confusion had held as his final gaze.
When in darkness, it's natural to search for the light,
And this was all there was on these sad, starless nights;
That was until, at around 2am,
On a windy night - who knows when -
Headlamps lit up Hate's weary frame from behind.
Stones and sand bounced as a groaning rumble
Announced itself from further back,
Followed by a horn that hacked
Through the white noise of the desert air,
Before blasting once more as it ascended to where
Hate was mindlessly zigzagging over a road.
A few seconds later, the force sent him
Stumbling ankle over toe onto the verge
As a mega-trailer truck emerged at his side,
With its time-hardened driver sitting up high.
"Where you headed?" came the plain, low voice
Of the trucker.
Yet, in silence, Hate didn't acknowledge
His attempt to succour
And carried on up the road,

CHAPTER XIV

While the truck crawled beside him pulling its load.

Tr: Well, wherever you're going,
      You won't reach it soon,
      Unless what you're after is another
      Thousand miles of sand dunes.
      Even then, apparently they've just given the orders;
      They're about to resume the airstrikes and mortars.

The truck's engine noise filled the air until,

H: I'm going nowhere.
Tr: Aren't we all...
      If it's all the same to you,
      Why don't you help keep me awake?
      I've got a cargo load of food for the refugees' sake.
      I'm still a long way off but it may as well arrive,
      And if you stay out here much longer,
      I reckon you'll die.
H: I have a suspicion Death might not comply
      With such a request.
Tr: Well, while you're waiting, may I suggest
      You hop on board?
      I'm just a stranger, nothing more.

CHAPTER XV

Not a word was spoken into the dawn,
And through the pit stops and piss stops
The silence carried on;
On through the heat of the midday rays
While the trucker tried to suss the tormenting maze
Within his passenger's mind.
It was something of himself he recognised in kind.

Tr: The problem with the voices in your head
   Is that they only ever see the world
   Through your own eyes.

Hate blinked his first blink in days.

H: You would think then that we might recognise
   Ourselves in our own reflection.
Tr: It just goes to show how little they know.
   They have a habit of blocking out others' perceptions.
H: Sometimes for the better.
Tr: Sometimes for the worse.
   The art of Self-Loathing is a cognitive curse.

"If you say so," Hate replied, ready to welcome
Silence back once more;
But the trucker knew the game, he'd been there before.

CHAPTER XV

Tr: *What's weighing on your mind?*
H: *...I'm completely empty.*
Tr: *And yet somehow emptiness can feel so heavy.*
       To feel nothing, we believe, is surely not to care
       Until we realise we've left the door open for Despair,
       And then wonder how long she's been sitting there.
       At least she reminds us that we are still alive.
H: *Such is her cruelty, for failure to make her leave*
       Is to make you wish to die.
Tr: *Seems like you've met her before.*
       How did you escape her then?
H: *I made companions of Anger and Revenge.*
Tr: *And where are they now?*
H: *I ran out of energy to keep them as friends.*
       The last I heard, Revenge made office,
       With a seat at the table.
Tr: *He will steal the role of Justice wherever he's able.*
H: *Justice is dead. I watched him get shot.*
Tr: *You've seen your fair share of the war then,*
       Have you not?

Hate felt his mind fly backwards in reflection
Through a wind of flashbacks
Swelling in violent resurrection against his will.
To close his eyes was like standing in a darkroom
Watching still after still surface in disturbing clarity,
Revealing each twisted image of ruthless brutality;
The photographs of memory that can never be erased,
As if Truth still held his currency from beyond the grave.

H: *I feel I have cursed this world with Hostility.*
Tr: *It was already cursed with Indifference.*

For all of your actions,
Never has there been a force more strong
Than that which recruits between the right and wrong
In complete silence,
An army of billions unaware of their alliance
To the disease that allows all others to spread.

H: *Since I was young, I've only ever seen*
The back of his head.
It was years before I discovered my hate for his name.

Tr: *And yet he eased your burden when Hostility came.*

H: *...Is our life no more than a senseless quest*
For futile answers, being guided by Blame?

*Blame

Tr: *Blame, the spineless orator impervious to Shame,*
Promoting himself as our best protection
When his only worth is in self-reflection.
We employ him to rail against the system's faults
Which profits each time in his profitless assaults.
Blame was a pauper once,
Before quickly making his fortune writing
The narratives where you are nothing but the hero,
Story after story commissioned by Ego.
You'd be surprised how often we entrust him
With the wealth of our integrity:
That we are always the victim, never the abuser;
That we stand with Truth in the role of the accuser;
So consumed with a reputation to protect
We become hostage to the pretensions we posture
And the platitudes we perfect.
The values we wear he uses

CHAPTER XV

To absolve our responsibility, duty and care
When the weight of the world is too much to bear.
We have all had dark days;
We have all made mistakes;
But perhaps the greatest of all
Is refusing to live with the choices we make.
He is the fool's mentor;
The student of Blame
Robs himself of the power to ever learn or change.

H: *By that logic, we are a civilisation of fools.*
For, at one point or another,
He has schooled us all in our false certainty.
If the seeds of Blame were to grow into corn,
We could feed this world for eternity.

Tr: *Wouldn't that be something?*
...So where are you headed?

H: *I don't know.*
Wherever the first signs of light or life are hiding.

Tr: *Well, I've got five refugees in the back*
Heading to a camp where Hospitality's residing?

H: *If she knew who I was, she wouldn't let me pass.*

Tr: *I wouldn't be so sure,*
She pays no heed to status or class.
Never has. I respect her for that.
But if you have different plans,
The Capital is the next city we hit.
Well, I say city, at least what's left of it.
It's a ruin of the culture and commerce it once was,
A bombsite of bricks, order and law.
The only thriving life still serving its cause
Is that of the printing press, still fueling a war
With propaganda and deceit

> *To line the pockets of the rich and elite*
> *Who dine with arms dealers,*
> *Projecting profit and loss,*
> *While the soldiers and civilians suffer the true cost*
> *As they sleep and wake with the horrors of our age,*
> *And cry for loved ones over newly dug graves.*
> *Go there if you want but I'm not sure what you'll find.*

H: *It's as good a place as any.*

Tr: *Your choice, not mine.*
> *We should be there by nine.*

They carried on driving into the late afternoon;
And when the sun finally gave up waiting on the moon
It abandoned them once again into black,
With nothing but their headlamps and occasional cracks
Of mortars flashing far off
To light their way as they landed soft
Just beyond the approaching Capital.
It looked almost unnatural in its blacked-out form;
A victim of the storms it could no longer weather
After the last strands of Concord
Had been completely severed.
Meanwhile, Chaos and Insanity remained tethered
To the last posts of a concrete wreckage patrolled by ghosts.

As they neared, the truck advanced
With the headlights turned off.

Tr: *Well, this is nearly your stop.*
> *If you don't mind, I'd rather not get caught*
> *In the city centre's hell.*
> *There's a spot I can drop you at on the outer belt*

	Where we won't be seen.
H:	*Whatever you think is fine for me.*
Tr:	*Wherever you go, I hope you find home eventually.*
H:	*I don't have a home.*
Tr:	*...We all have a home;*
	Only some of us spend our whole life trying to find it.
H:	*While the rest spend their life*
	Trying to somehow redefine it.
Tr:	*You'll know it when you find it.*
H:	*You reckon?*
	How do we know what we're looking for?
	At this rate, we'll be lucky to find
	Four walls and a door.
Tr:	*Don't confuse bricks and stone*
	As the place our hearts seek as home.
	We can lay our head on the same bed for years,
	Yet it's those beside us that give shelter from our fears.
H:	*Don't make your home the heart of another;*
	They will leave eventually and it's you who'll suffer
	As your home caves in.
Tr:	*Just as houses can at the strength of the wind.*
	The foundations are stronger when laid within.
H:	*And more painful when they break.*
Tr:	*Yeah, there's truth in that,*

*The Search For Home

In this world we can't ever completely rely,
And with Hope and Faith we do our best to try.
Yet, from me to you and the infinite stars,
Tribulation flies recklessly, near and far.
But somewhere in this world

*Is the home for your heart and the shelter
We seek from the elements of life.
And you will know it when you find it:
It's where you will sit in stillness,
And your mind will be at peace,
And the voices in your head
Will cease with their grief;
Where you can grow in the soil of your soul
And absorb your joys and pains, like sun and rain,
As nourishment and strength to see each day anew -
For new sights with old eyes prove a colourless view;
Where you can believe your presence
Is not where you're seen
But in the hearts of those who,
In that moment, are unseen;*

*Where you shatter the illusion
That you are in this world alone,
That's when you will know
You have found your home.
...And you take it wherever you go.*

The truck slowed to a halt, then the engine killed,
And once more the nighttime air was filled
With unnerving quiet and a dusty haze.
Yet, despite the potential danger,
Hate seemed completely unphased;
His thoughts were still hanging
On the trucker's final words.

Tr: We're just on the outskirts of the east side of town.
       If you find the canal you can follow it

CHAPTER XV

> *All the way down to the central square,*
> *Though, if I were you, I wouldn't stay there.*

H: *What's next for you after your journey's done?*

Tr: *I don't know. Guess I'll see where the next turn*
> *In the road takes me.*

Hate looked at the trucker and took in his face;
Two strangers in a world
Where only strangers were commonplace.
Yet, Hate wondered if he had somehow made a friend
In a time where friendships seemed to meet short, cruel ends.
He said nothing.
He opened the door and jumped down onto the grass,
And went round to the driver's side to take one last look
At his short-lived acquaintance.

Tr: *Well, thanks for your company.*
> *In the absence of any working radio stations*
> *You were a welcome find.*
> *Perhaps we'll meet again sometime*
> *When this pointless war meets its pointless end.*

H: *Where is home for you?*

Tr: *...In all honesty, I don't have a clue.*
> *Thirty years in this truck and still searching,*
> *It's all I can do.*
> *I'll find it someday.*

H: *What's your name?*

Tr: *Loneliness.*

Then the engine awoke and the truck pulled away.

CHAPTER XVI pt. I

Hate had been rooted to the spot
After watching the one spirit he thought
Might be his only true friend in this world
Disappear into nowhere;
Into the mercy of Future and Chance,
Like our connections in life that are gone at a glance.
Then into the depths of the city he advanced,
With no plans but to take up the suggestion
And follow the direction of the creeping canal;
Walking in plain sight with the cold rationale
That if Death was to stay true to his threat,
He had nothing to fear from whoever he met.
He walked for an hour past half-sunken boats,
Whose bows gasped for air in sinking respect
Alongside the tents, once homes of last hope,
Drowning in the reeds in barren neglect.

Eventually, he came up onto a bridge...
And held his breath at the jaw-dropping sight.
His eyes momentarily blinked and twitched
At the revelation of Devastation's ruthless might.
Half-buildings stood like broken staircases
Ascending to a hopeless drop,
While foundations of furniture stood like
Stakes in the ground,
Like a splintering forest through which Hate walked.

CHAPTER XVI pt. I

His footsteps stumbled over broken roof slate
That buried the remains of the possessions
Of all those that put their faith in Fate,
Before being blitzed by the bombs of Aggression.
And then, just as he managed to find his footing,
He felt a coldness beneath his feet.
He looked down to find he was standing on a street
Paved with gravestones,
Engraved with loving memories to give life
To all those who now lay lifeless beneath him.
All those who had fallen,
For right or for wrong,
To the rhythm of war and its mournful song,
But, regardless, were now irretrievably gone,
Now made a road of harrowing history.
Meanwhile, living loved ones are left to pray,
In the realms of mystery,
For a life beyond our own
Where those we miss now laugh and play
In happiness and grace.

Hate felt his heart shift and displace,
Treading lightly up Death's slab-made path.
On every step, he read another grieving epitaph,
Words we hope will be the eternal reminder
For the next generation who choose the road of conflict
To reach their destination.
The path led all the way into the central square and beyond,
Right through to the slums where Hate once played -
The slums of SpiritLand which Hate once called home.
But where is home for the heart that beats for nothing?
Regardless, the city was only itself in shadow and memory.

In reality, it had become a concrete cemetery
Of its former existence, as Loneliness had described.
And off in the distance, Hate could already hear
The smash of wrecking balls, the rumble of diggers,
The rise of cranes that got bigger and bigger.
The new world leaders were roaring up their machines
To build their new world, gross and obscene.
They were already fighting over positions elected,
Already voting to have their new wealth protected,
And soon they'd be fighting over the size
Of their statues erected.
It had been out with the old and in with the new,
But Corruption had managed to survive the coup
And reinstate himself as Chief Adviser
To a new group of ministers, none the wiser
To the sway of Temptation, Power and Greed -
And how easily one's want takes over our need.
And just as he'd promised, back in his youth,
Pride Jr was there in office, high up,
In a brand new jacket and plush, polished boots;
So near the top, he'd forgotten his roots.

But back in the ruins of the old city square
Hate looked around as if he could feel Despair nearby...
But he was completely alone...
Alone but for a hatred
That was chewing him to his bones.
But hatred for what?
Even the tower and the old town clock
Had been destroyed -
As if Time had fled the city
And caught the last plane going west

To try and retrieve the day before the dawn of the conquest.
All Hate could see was a world black and grey -
A world where even Grief surely wouldn't want to stay.
And then, out of nowhere,
In complete confusion and maddening disarray,
Hate let out a scream that rang so viciously through the air
It shattered the glass of Heaven
And caught the Gods unaware
As their walls started to crumble and crack.

H: *Confusion! If you can hear me,*
I have a truth for you:
In our lives, there is no going back.

And with those words, a tear broke from Hate's eye,
As if a vault of remorse, hidden deep inside,
Had fractured at its edge.
A moment later, drops of water fell on his head,
Followed by a deafening crack of thunder that severed the sky
And released a monsoon as Hate started to cry,
As if the world might drown in his tears
And drown him with them.
With nothing left in life to hate,
All that was left for Hate in life
Was to hate himself.
With the last hint of conviction left in his being,
He was now determined to escape the world
Behind the all-seeing eyes of Death;
To break through fire exit doors of life without the key
And simply cease to be.
Stumbling helplessly through the deluge of his pain,
He came across an object,

Floating down a river of rain -
A rope -
The faithful friend to those who can't cope.
All he needed now was his own gentle gallows,
One last request in his journey unhallowed.
Like a prisoner escaping to his freedom,
He scaled the scree of the old cathedral hall
Which raised him to a lamppost still standing tall
Amongst this vista of Ruination.
"I am in control of my own creation,"
He said through gritted teeth,
As he knotted the rope to the rain-soaked metal.

H: *It's time to settle this final score*
       With a mind that deserves nothing more
       Than man or spirit deserve the forgiveness of nature;
       Time to leave this land and meet my maker.

Adjusting the length of his rope,
He slipped the noose around his throat
And took one last look down towards
The raging torrents below.
Between him and the water
He knew there was an abyss
Into which his soul would fall,
And leave his hanging body lifeless.
He crawled his way out to the lamppost's head,
His hands and face being lashed by the rain
As if the weather agreed with his own disdain.
With his body wrapped around the steel
He tried to dredge up the courage to let go.

H: *Don't let my father visit me now.*
      Hell, keep the voice of Fear down below.
      Keep him mute and gagged by the dead!

And then, as if the waves slowed,
The image of his mother came into his head.
And just like a baby ceasing to cry
When its heart feels the parent's embrace,
Hate suddenly seemed excited to die,
Knowing Purity lay beyond the gates.
And with that thought, his arms released.
Slowly he fell through the storm's raging beast,
The rope spiralling towards its taut execution,
Holding Hate's life as the price for the world's restitution.
Hate was falling with grace, three, two, ONE...

SMASH!

A lightning bolt shot into the lamppost's shin.
Hate's gallows keeled
Moments before the afterlife was revealed.
The rope coiled and spun
As Hate's body plummeted into the river running
Violently through the city's burnt skeleton.
It dragged him under, through its current apace,
Before spitting him out in horrid distaste
Against disjointed bollards and jagged rocks.
Hate surfaced, gasping in life's putrid air
As if the afterlife had rejected his entry and mocked.

H: *Death! Let me die!*
      Let me die!

At least do me the service of hearing my cry!
Take me to a place where someone's hate
Is greater than my own.
Take me to where violence and punishment
Are nothing but condoned!
Take me out of this life!
Take me to where I can feel the cold steel
Of the knife of Justice at my neck.
Take revenge on the wreck of my soul
In a place where the ghosts of Repentance
Don't haunt one's heart!

At that moment, the hail started to part...
To reveal the haze of light he had followed so far.
No longer in haze but shining through the dark,
Hate spotted the flickering soft glow
Spilling out from a singular apartment window
In the middle of a battered, beaten, abandoned block -
A light shining with hope in a city Hate believed
Only Hopelessness now walked.
Across the water he swam,
Across to the third floor of the building.
He clambered in and began
To ascend the ruined staircase -
Then stopped...
Caught in a feeling these steps were being re-traced...
He looked down at the old wooden boards;

H: *Is this a trick of the mind?*
       Another trick of mind and Time,
       The deja vu's that jolt our rhythms and rhymes?

He had never climbed this stairwell,
Yet, for the second time in his life,
He felt he'd passed this way before
And what's more, somehow knew
Who resided on the other side of the door,
Two floors up.
No matter how far we travel or try to escape,
Over guilty seas and roads shamefully shaped,
The anchor of our conscience
Will inevitably bring us back to the heart;
The mind finally gives up
And can no longer run
Under the weight of our toils.
He ascended the stairs as if already
Walking into the next world,
Surrendering his soul to the unknown.
And while the whirl and burl of the storm raged outside,
Hate's inner tempest of purpose and pride
Began to slow, wane, then abruptly subside,
Before the waters of sadness began to flood him inside
As he approached the door.
Here he stood,
As if Future had done all that Future could,
And with nothing left to give,
Handed Present back the clock.

...Knock.

...Silence.

...The door creaked open on its hinge...

Hate saw an old spirit staring back at him.
She looked tired,
Her hair wisping grey,
Her eyes bearing the weight of a past
Too much to relay in one lifetime.
Yet, though she had aged way beyond her years,
Every contour of her face was true and sincere.
Every smile of joy, every frown of grief,
Every grit of conviction from every heart-made belief
Was there to be read on her weathered skin,
Burrowing deep into the chasms of her countenance within.
And although they had never met,
They stood there in such deep connect,
Recognising every aspect of each other's being,
As if they lived within each other as DNA unseen.
Hate now had nothing left to fight with
But the honesty of his past.
Yet, unknowingly, he had disarmed the old spirit
Who was hiding behind a mask
Of quiet courage and assuring grace.
Within, memories she had spent years putting to sleep
Were suddenly stirring in fearful wake
As she looked upon a ghost in Hate's nervous face -
A ghost from back in a happier day,
When Youth cared not for tomorrow.
Then Hate breathed in...

And the whole world stopped

And listened....

CHAPTER XVI pt. I

Hate's Confession

H: My name is Hate.
I am the bastard son of Fear after he gave up on Love.

I am a leader to millions who have risen to my words,
I resurrected the strength of the deprived and the hurt.
I found victims silenced by Cruelty's hand
And victims of Violence, exploited and damned,
The victims cheated when their rights were wronged,
The victims seeking recompense
But ignored in their throngs;
I made bullets of their tears,
The same self-made metal I used to kill Fear.
And as brothers in arms they raged
With the courage of Spite...
Now please hear the confession for the sins of my life.

I have walked with Jealousy and bolstered his cause,
I sat with Envy in glee;
I told the beggar we would rewrite the laws
And promised I could set him free.
I stole the speech of Retribution
And harnessed the voice of the crowd,
Then score upon score marched in Hate's revolution
And the voice of Revenge rang aloud.
And if ever Doubt came into the fray
I brought Pride right to the front,
And with Integrity's cloak he'd masquerade
With the rhetoric of Honour on his tongue.
I gave Anger the strength of unknown might,
Then teamed him with Madness and Rage,

*And when Destruction came in joyful delight
I watched the riots take centre stage -
I watched as Anarchy tore up the town,
And while Reason was lynched by the mob;
And when Chaos came to burn the whole country down
I gave Justice credit for the job.
And in the name of Justice, I gave rise to Pain,
In the name of Justice we bled;
When the walls were graffitied with Sanity's blood,
"In the name of Justice" we read.
In the name of Justice, Innocence fell
To the sounds of bullets and bombs;
And we called them collateral and casualties of war,
And then blindly carried on.
In the name of Justice, I made martyrs of the meek
Who fought for false purpose of life;
From kindness to killing, all those who were willing
Fell in the midst of their strife.
And in the name of Justice, we made Dignity watch
As we pillaged and plundered the dying;
Then, in a ransacked village, we let Dignity rot
And left our flag of Justice a' flying.
In the name of Justice, Forgiveness was gagged;
In darkness I held her in chains
And left her to starve to a bundle of rags
As a prisoner of Hate's domain.*

*I am the killer of Grace,
The absolver of Wrath,
A keeper of trials and ills of the past.
I am Pity's worst foe,
Temper's so-called friend;*

I am the open wound that Time can't mend.
I am the butcher of Reason,
I am the maker of lies
To sharpen the knives of Vengeance and Pride.
I am the crusher of Solace,
The oppressor of Joy,
I am the quiet unrest you wish to destroy.
I am the voice in your head
That craves one's respect
And will kill for the ego I live to protect.
I am the maker of suffering,
I am the teacher of pain,
I made students of Loathing, Scorn and Disdain.
I let Modesty hang,
I watched Trust drown,
I smiled as Decorum was mauled by the hounds.
I fed fear to one race,
Injustice to another,
Then let blood spill for religion and colour.
I watched Torture dance
On the backs of the frightened
Like an ignorant child with dreams of a titan.
I watched streets swarm
With Brutality's rave;
The good and the guiltless stained the paves
As Terror and Dread,
Bathed in red,
Scythed the weak as they desperately fled.
And I found the only survivors
At Kindness's side
As she lay there helpless, with nothing to hide.
I led the way of Ignorance,

I had Understanding condemned,
I built the wall between the Us and the Them.
I stand as a leader
But am no more than a child
Lost in a blackness spreading out for miles.
I've known only two friends,
Loneliness and Confusion,
The latter found Insanity to grant his own absolution
And escaped a world
So filled with hate
That the earth is sinking under my weight.

But for all the actions that have left their scars
There is one that has left the gardens of my heart
So exposed to the winds of Regret
That it batters and blows until there is nothing left
Upon which new plants can grow.
As if, one by one, I have smothered the glow
Of night-time's guiding lights,
Until I know not which way to go to find shelter
In the hour of my soul's desperate fright...

I killed Compassion.

I left her lifeless on her back.
I let her soul rise up to the cold night sky
And, in an instant, all was black
As I watched her spirit extinguish
The last two stars lighting our way;
The stars of Reconciliation and Redemption.

I am not worthy of one's forgiveness

CHAPTER XVI pt. I

And thus only wish to ask one question -
Was this always to be me?
Was this always to be my destiny
Or did I wield my own choice?
Are we but shooting stars in the night
Or is our course mapped out in the sky?
In death will I learn the meaning of life
Or learn it was all a meaningless lie?
Was it all pre-made, this part I played,
Or did I choose my own evens and odds?
Or were my joys and pain no more than
Chips in a game of roulette
Between Fate and the Gods?

In those words, a single tear ran down Love's cheek.
How twisted a world that won't let your past sleep.
Every line of Hate's confession
Was like a dagger through Love's breast
As if something, somewhere, will never cease to test
The ever-fragile strength of our nature as it bends and blows
Like a reed in the wind.
But even as the strings of her heart stretched to break,
She did what only Love can for the sake
Of love when love is pure.
She endured.
She endured every stab of honesty
And aching blow from the hands
Of a child simply desperate to know
The "whys" and "why nots"
In a world where answers are as rare
As a unicorn's breath echoing in the air.
Then the silence broke as Love stepped away from the door

And invited Hate into her home.
But Hate's feet remained stuck to the floor
As he felt a feeling he had never known.
As if being killed by a kindness
He knew not how to receive,
Hate feared, at any moment, he would buckle at the knees.
"Come in," Love gently said.

H: *I do not deserve the roof of your name.*
L: *That's only true if we hold value in Blame*
        And seek only to absolve ourselves of fault
        And care not for the source of Morality's assault.
        Come in and take shelter from the storm.

Hate hesitantly stepped through
Into the warmth of the room,
But, in doing so, any courage left was consumed
By another wave of guilt
As he looked upon families of the homeless,
Wrapped in blankets and quilts,
Huddled together all the way up the hall,
As if Love's door had been open to shelter one and all.
He turned to the kitchen to see more on the other side -
Never before had he felt such deep divide.
As he looked at the migrants' clothes
He thought he saw those he knew;
Their countenance took him back
To the days of his youth
And all the dispirited spirits who lived with nothing,
Only now it was Hate who was the cause of their suffering.
He, once famed as the one True Son,
Was now seeing the consequence of all that had been done;

He, once proclaimed as the Chosen Son,
Was lost for an answer to what he'd become.

H: I am a spirit this world does not need,
       So why am I here?
       I never asked to be the son of Fear.
L: That we are brought into the world unclear of why
       Is a suffering we must live with until the day we die.
       How we nurture that suffering is all we can decide,
       For the pulse of our temperament
       Beats within the hearts of sleeping wolves
       That hide in the forest of our nature.
       We are not purely fear,
       We are not purely hate,
       We are not purely love
       Nor one single trait.
       We are a pack of all
       And each must be fed to find its place,
       From the wolf of anger
       To the wolf of grace.
       Yet, each one you wake
       Will determine the choices and actions you take
       To rise against the tribulation of the time.
       And therein lies the future of your prime.
       Each time stirred, the wolf will sleep light,
       Hoping to be woken and fed for the fight.
       The ones we feed full are the ones that thrive.
       The stronger they grow,
       The stronger their will to survive,
       Until we become the wolves we feed:
       From the wolf of greed
       Who will not be ignored

> *To the wolf of pride*
> *Who will lead us to war,*
> *To the wolf of hate,*
> *That unknowingly consumes us*
> *Right down to our core.*

H: *Then why did I have to wake in hatred?*
Why did Pride crave pride from birth?

L: *Pride has its place, it's the pride of self-worth;*
That we have our place and right to live on this earth,
Yet are no more or less than the
Smallest fragment of the universe
That plays its equal part in the cycle of life.
Believing we are greater is to be poisoned by our hype.
Pride too proud acts as a soldier of survival
Holding a rifle ready to backfire.

H: *And what of Hate?*
What of Fear?
Those who push away all that is dear
In favour of Ignorance, Destruction and Blame.

L: *You forget from whence your hatred first came.*
Yes, you are Hate,
The son of Fear,
But a child of Purity
Who saw the world unjudgingly clear.
You first railed against injustice
That slept on Poverty's streets
And cursed the apathy of the privileged and elite.
You saw the world from the tops of high-rise flats,
Looking back on a system that ruthlessly taxed
Your happiness and freedom to expand its own.
You saw the prejudice that widened class separation
And raged against Inequity and leaders' violations.

Anger harnessed can give us strength,
But Anger unleashed knows not the length of suffering,
And Anger spread knows no governing.
We can all fight for Justice,
But the weapons we use
Are what prove the metal of our dignity
In the eyes of Providence.

H: *Who cares for the Gods*
In whom we have lost all confidence?

*Where Have You Been?

And if love is the answer
Then where have you been?
It's not enough to say love simply exists
When you live on the streets where hardship persists.
A mother's love is not enough
In the ghettos where self-worth sleeps cold and rough
On the breadline borders between
The prosperous and the penniless.
So where have you been?
Compassion's words hold no weight
To those resigned to Poverty's fate.
And for those that are willing to fight the next day,
They are nothing more than a token grace
Recited indoors in irony and haste
Over their best attempt at a meal,
Earned in violence and merciless appeal.
Where have you been?
While you celebrate in the dance of two lovers' vows,
Misfortune weds itself to another growing crowd.
I wouldn't mind your absence

If I could afford the distractions
Like those who buy joys to hide their dissatisfactions,
But I grew up with those for whom
The entertainment of Denial
Was a luxury they couldn't afford,
So where have you been?
When the deprived turned to the aid of Jealousy,
Where were you?
When Greed stole the blind pauper's legacy,
Where were you?
When Anger stood for those with no job
And Prejudice was the one to brand them 'the mob',
When they lost their homes, were forced into shacks,
And held to ransom to buy their own rights back,
Where were you?
When Prosperity celebrated a nation that thrived
And hid Privation to cover his lies,
And then ate to excess and lay fat on the floor
While corpses of Starvation decayed next door,
Where were you?
When the broken mother found solace in drugs,
When the broken father found solace in Lust,
When the broken child found solace
In the crusts of stale bread
And children's books which would never be read,
Where were you?
Where have you been?
What good is love if love is unseen?
For every child born in your name
The orphans of love are born tenfold in vain.

L: *And do you think I don't feel their pain?*
As the world strains under the weight disowned,

*Do you think I don't hear the cries of those
Who believe they are in this world alone?*

H: *Well, if the power of love is so mighty and great
Why do millions put their faith in hate?*

L: *Because they have lost faith
In the inner strength of themselves.
Love is only strong when enough believe
It can right the wrongs.
But to fight with love
And to fight with forgiveness
Demands all the courage this world can give us.
For we must trust in our compassion,
Unclench our hands,
Let their anger rave
And try to understand
As we remain unguarded enough to say
'I have faith in the goodness and strength
Of your heart that you may find another way
Through the fears of your toil.'*

H: *What is the point, when we have created a living
That breeds inherent turmoil throughout our path?*

L: *Because if the Gods don't exist,
And Fate is a myth,
Then love and compassion are the only chance we have.*

H: *It's not enough.*

L: *It can be, if enough people trust...*

H: *And what happens when someone calls your bluff
On everything Love claims love can fulfil?*

L: *Then I will show my cards,
And you will see I never claimed
To offer more or less than true love's will.*

H: *Which is?*

True Love's Will

L: The will to care when anger rails,
The will to hope when hope has set sail.
The will to give time to those undeserving,
The will to not judge those of no learning.
The will to stop where others pass by
And have the courage to meet Poverty's eye,
And look upon the beggar in equal measure
And remember that integrity
Is our true wealth and treasure.
The will to believe that conflict and war
Will never find the loving peace we search for;
Yet when the horrors of futile madness burn bright,
To have the will to act for innocent lives.
The will to act when others have lost
And not stand by as Injustice walks.
The will to receive an orphan of love
And accept that their heart is yours to take care of.
The will to listen in one's hour of need
And the will to trust a friend with your grief.
The will to enjoy one's fortune graced
And not let jealousy take joy's place.
The will to look past one's faults and failings
And search for their virtues without comparing,
Then the will to accept an apology given,
And, though not be walked over, worse yet, not driven
By the strength of our ego and the sense of our pride
That holds back our forgiveness with all of its might.
The will to struggle through another's strife,
And, for that time, set aside the goals of your life.
And when all is done, not wait for debt repaid

*But hope it's paid forward in someone else's dark day.
The will to have patience through an addict's disdain
When they curse your existence
And say you're to blame;
And where some see a monster,
You recognise illness
And believe within them, though trapped,
Lives goodness.
The will to trust someone values your voice
And to help you through life is their greatest of joys,
And thus not be ashamed to need their aid
And know that true love
Takes more than one to be made.
And then the will to ceaselessly give and inspire
Long after sensation and pleasure have tired,
And not to confuse romance with love,
For only one has the foundations that here we speak of.
True love's will is to give your life for the few
That give meaning to your living and purpose anew,
For those you can't imagine your world without,
Who have stood by you in every moment of doubt,
For those with whom you have shared
The beauty of this earth,
And have shown you the true essence of your worth,
For those you hold in your protective embrace
When ill health drains the courage from their face.
And in the final hours,
In the last suffering moments,
We finally understand
That joy and pain
Live hand in hand.
True love's will is to watch our loved one*

Feel Death drawing nigh,
Yet believe that true love will always survive
In eternity;
And in quiet, peaceful serenity,
Trust, when we are gone,
Those we have touched will help true love live on.

Hate's defences were gone.
He was as powerless to the world
As the day he was born,
And all he could do was let the eyes of the innocent
Fall upon him in whatever judgement they may.
He looked at Love,
And behind her, on the wall,
Hung a photo of her happier day:
Smiling, with the arms of her husband
Wrapped around her waist;
The arms of a father Hate never embraced,
With a smiling face alien to Hate's memory.
"He loved you," Hate uttered in a weak voice.

H: *His love for you was matched*
        Only by his love for Regret in losing you.
        He never cried for another.

L: *I cried a river of tears for your mother.*
        I only wish that could've brought her back.
        I wish I had been stronger
        When my life crumbled through its cracks.
        I wish that I had chased your mum when
        She ran from this flat with you in her womb.
        I searched for you by day and by the light of the moon,
        But to no avail.

H: She hid us from society and Reputation's trail.
        You would never have found us.
        If you want to beat the ransom of Shame,
        Simply set up shop where no one cares for your name;
        Where Reputation is forgotten over the preoccupation
        Of finding another quick fix
        To help you forget that your life is in bits.
        Your words could barely find their way to that slum,
        Nevermind yourself.
        And any words that come,
        It's as if they're being tested in the fires of Hell.
        Love is not taught there,
        It's only brought there by those who have
        Experienced it in a former life elsewhere.
        Patience and Charity used to be there apparently
        But I was too young to remember.

CHAPTER XVI pt. II

There was a peaceful calm in the air
As Love and Hate spoke candidly on this occasion so rare.
The soft tones in their words had lulled
The last of Love's lodgers into a restful sleep
And their silences shared for moments of thought
Suggested a trust had been forged in this time to keep.
"Did you really believe it was true love?" Hate asked,
In a voice gentle and kind.

L: Yes...I think I did.
        I was naive when I was young,
        I would give myself to Passion
        And fly too close to the sun,
        Only to be burnt at the end of the fling
        And then do it again and again,
        Never learning.
        And then I met Fear, so timid and shy,
        Afraid of taking the first step
        For fear it would die.
        But for all of his caution, he wasn't naive,
        Like me. I could believe it was meant to be -
        That Fear would keep me grounded,
        And I could let Fear see
        A world where Honesty lives,
        And Forgiveness governs,
        And where openness makes our conflicts less stubborn.

*For unknowns are unknown only because
We don't understand.
And I said to Fear, "Let's try,"
Then gently took his hand.
And we danced.
We danced to the tune of Romance through the years
And despite his disposition, he killed my fears
Of ever being alone in this world again.
We were a team; able to fight anything...
Or so it seemed.
Within his embrace, and the smile on his face,
He would hold my heart in all its vulnerability,
Like a broken-winged bird
Delicately cupped in the hand.
But even with love, Life can make other plans.*

H: *He believed he couldn't be
All he thought he had to be.
He thought by leaving you he would set you free.
So scared of love, he chose to deny,
Then so scared of losing you, he chose to lie;
So scared of the unknown, he chose to fly.
And despite everything he did I can understand why.
To truly love is to tempt the greatest of suffering.
Is it really worth the risk?*

L: *Is the suffering of life worth it if its greatest gifts
We choose to miss?*

There they were, Love and Hate,
Standing in a stalemate
In a game impossible to win or lose,
Where the only power we have is to choose
What to do with the time laid upon our hands

As the collisions of each other's rights and wrongs
Alter the course we otherwise may have planned.
And as Love and Hate stood in opposition,
In the corner of their vision was the ghost of Fear.
And as Fear looked to Love,
As Love looked at Hate,
As Hate felt Fear,
Hovering near was the ghost of Purity,
Holding her son's hand,
As he began to accept he was in a world
He could never truly understand.

H: *What do I do now? Where can I go?*
My mind still longs for the hyenas
That can tear a hole in my body
Large enough to let my grief drain away,
For it would take a lifetime and a day
For my well of regret to empty through my eyes alone.
Yet I believe that Death will not let me leave
Even into the gates of Hell,
And my conscience is not yet ready to walk these streets
Where so many fell and now lie buried
Under the ashes of Mercy.

L: *Leave here.*
Leave this city and all you think it holds:
Your reputation, your desires,
And all the importance you've acquired,
Leave it all and walk free.
The relationships worth having,
Though they may bleed, they will survive the time.
For now, put them to the back of your mind
And walk blind to Future

And awake to Present,
And accept that we are all forever adolescents
As you let Mother Nature guide your spirit back
To a place of peace and tranquillity.
Cast aside your instability and simply
Breathe in rhythm with the breath of the earth;
Take time to be,
Take time to feel,
Take the time with Nature to let your heart heal.

H: *Where does one go to find such a refuge from Life*
While still being forced to breathe her air?

*The Journey Home

L: *As you escape from underneath the clouds,*
Laced in thick smog as they hang and shroud
The tops of tower blocks that stand dead to their view,
The din of the city will soften around you
As the hiss of the angry exhaust-fume snake,
And the scream of the sirens that pierce
Through the headache, fall and drift away.
The bark of the dog, the moan of the cat,
The wailing of armies of mice and rats
Will fade into echoes as you leave
The decaying streets of the ghettos
And drift onwards towards the townships of shacks
That bake and dissipate in the heat of the outback.

From there may your journey begin,
With no other voice than that of the wind
To accompany you.
As you walk out into the desert,

Where the dunes make the horizon roll and wave,
And arid cliffs redirect your way,
And as the ground ripples and weaves its tracks
Sideways towards the edge of the earth,
Feel each grain of sand under your feet
And know, regardless of how tiny and light,
Collectively they have the strength and might
To swallow you whole without trace.
Acknowledge your place.
Yet, allow the ghost of Courage to hover nearby.
The vultures that circle overhead are not for you.
But go lightly where you tread,
For one's path is another's grave
And both deserve respect
For the part they have played.
Go softly past the bones that lay.
And when you feel lost, and the thoughts in your mind
Drift deliriously in and out of your past,
Notice the humble, scorched grass -
Golden, it camouflages against
The backdrop of sand.
For these unassuming reeds,
Resilient to the night's bite
And the day's relentless heat,
Will guide you towards greener land
And lead you to the gift of the spring -
The watering hole that bestows life upon everything
In sight and reflects our honest countenance -
Our figure that has nothing to fight for
But our own survival as we exist on Nature's terms.
At this point feel grateful for life still given
And gratitude learned.

And as you reemerge from the water,
Cleansed and cradled in Mother Nature's arms,
Look towards the savannah,
With its vast, fair, sweeping plains,
Where roam the wildlife only ever tamed
By the tides of the moon and the burning of the sun
Which, fire-red, sets and silhouettes
The lion's head,
The elephant's tusk,
The giraffe's neck as it
Reaches up to the canopy of the flat-top trees
That stand haloed in golden light.
As you pass through the grasslands by day and night
Becoming the wandering nomad,
Absorb the sights,
For though we may not know the meaning of life
We have been gifted with the ability
To take joy and delight
In this masterpiece of creation,
So beyond our imagination
That, were the Gods to give us all the answers,
We would not know their use.
For, in our so-called wisdom,
We still cannot help but abuse
The powers and knowledge upon us granted -
We are but fools who forget we leave this world
Empty-handed.
As you walk through the plains,
With the buffalo, the antelope,
And all that do the same,
Pick up the soil, feel it slip through your fingers,
And accept that not even the dirt is yours to own -

We are but travellers sharing the same home
As our souls pass seamlessly as time
Through one universe to the next.

Eventually, you'll meet the river that connects
The crystal-capped mountains
To the diamond shimmering sea
That swirls in enchanting motion
And travels free towards the deep, unknown,
Magical blue expanse of the ocean.
And though the river's main body
May look sure and swift,
Choose a gentler fork through which to drift.
You are in no rush,
Know not your destination,
And your mind too fragile
To face the deep blue's reputation.
For this thing of beauty, so calm and so still,
Can turn so vicious of its own free will
And drag you out helpless, strand you without hope,
Then batter you senseless as you grasp for a rope
That will never float your way.
For, even at our strongest,
We are nothing to the waves.
Instead, choose the river
That has guessed its way through the glens
And meditates the forest as it meanders and bends
In patience and tranquillity;
Give yourself to the river
In all your vulnerability.
Lean back, let it carry you gently downstream,
And as the arching foliage dapples the light

CHAPTER XVI pt. II

In a thousand shades of green,
Let your ears submerge,
Become deaf to the world,
And float weightless
In these sheltered moments serene.

And from then, as you drift through the woodlands
And their mystical domain,
The climates and colours will around you change
Until, like a secret of the forest,
The last trees reveal the titanic mountain range
That surrounds you in majesty -
The sleeping giants that transcend our fantasy
As we stand upon them as weightless as a fly
Upon the back of a hand.
From here, begin your climb.
With each step, feel the heather
That slowly inclines up the hill
And spreads soft for miles as it
Humbly fills the wilderness
In a thousand purple shades,
And clothes the mountain of timeless age;
The mountain that once burned hot in molten rage
But now stands tall in accepting grace
Against the winds of Time that weather its face
And erodes its bones of water-worn stone.
And if ever worry blows against you as you walk,
Listen gently and hear the mountain talk
In all of its voice.
From the rumble of the burn that passes beneath
To the clicks and the hums that buzz around your feet,
From the gentle breeze that whistles through the rock

To the rustle of fern leaves that cling to their stalks,
To the song of the skylark as you ascend to its height,
To where creatures live,
Yet remain unseen
To those who take life as their sporting right;
To those who uproot the soil for wealth and gain
And will happily see the earth's blood drained
Until its wounds crust dry,
And our unity with Nature has no choice
But to die.
As you pass the home of the mountain hare
And feel the chill and thinning of the air,
Cast your eyes towards the peak
Where, in mutual respect, earth and sky meet
As the cloud brushes over its crown.
While navigating the ridge,
Feel the gentle sounds of silence surround you -
You will know the spirit of the earth
Has finally found you
As your lungs begin to cleanse
And your heart starts to mend.
Reach the mountain's top...
Stop...
Feel your breath suspend...
Here is a world whose beauty has no end
And, since the day you were born,
Has held you in its heart.
Take in the size of it all.
To feel so great yet be so small,
Allow your self-made illusion to fall
And stand exposed and awake to the truth
We try so hard not to know:

In the eyes of the universe, we are dust.
Yet, by the grace of Nature,
We are still privileged enough,
As if each particle of light,
That has been travelling before the dawn of time,
Has travelled down our own God-made leyline
To light up the wonders of the world for us to see
In every thread of colour weaved through its tapestry.
What joys we miss as we foolishly insist
On our self-importance.
And when loneliness swells from the depths of your soul
And you believe that you are nothing at all,
And the floods of grief well up in your eyes,
Do not hold back.
Let your soul cry -
Your tears of worthlessness will have found their worth
By the time your cheeks dry.
For to sit with loneliness and yet befriend the view
Is to surely be at one with peace and solitude.

And in this solitude
May you reflect on who you are,
With the failures and mistakes
That you have carried thus far.
The bags of guilt that weigh us
We hold not to discard,
But to look inside with honest acceptance
And learn from our errors.
The strongest in this life are not those without sin
But the grace-fallen souls that could look deep within
And feel the measure of their own mistake.
To touch the ashes of flames that forced the spirit break

And meet the eyes of our guilt,
This is the courage it takes to truly heal.
And in that healing comes our strength to feel
Love, forgiveness and compassion once more.

And when the time feels right,
From your newfound home,
With your newfound strength,
May you then cast your eyes
Beyond the beauty of the light
And back towards the storms and thunders
Of our own making
That rumble in your past life.
For, although the cleansed soul
May remain pure in clean air,
We must still test our strength
Amidst the despair of others,
For a saint is no one without sisters and brothers.
Learn forgiveness of oneself,
Learn forgiveness of others,
And in love may we return to all those who suffer.

EPILOGUE

Hate left that night, took Love's direction
And walked east towards the morning light and beyond.
And I, for one, no longer know where he is.
Some say they have felt him lurking in the shadows and mists
Of their darkening days,
While others tell tales of meeting him on crossroads
Before heading their separate ways.
Some believe he is still in the forest,
To others, still on the mountain peak
Taking in the colours of the grass and the flowers
That withstood the winter's temper bleak,
Before returning through spring
In a gracious patience that, never-ending,
Sends a marvelling rapture through Hate's heart.
Yet, some are certain he is back playing the part
They believe he was always meant to play;
Believing he will find them and lead them away
To the dark cave of the mind
That will protect them from trust -
That deception so unjust
That injured them once before.
They yearn for his strength and skill at shutting doors
Against the pain of Forgiveness
And the suffering of Second-Chance.
Despite all those whom Love and Compassion have saved,
There are still millions who believe

In a solace Hate grants.
And I can understand why:
For what a thankless task showing love can seem
When Life is forcing you to cry.
Yet, that darkness, as I once heard Hate say,
Smothers the glow of night-time's guiding lights,
Until you know not which way to go to find shelter
In the hour of your soul's desperate fright.

Now, I think I should say...
When I first told this tale,
A couple of questions arose
Which I feel I should address before I go.
Questions the reader may not feel compelled to ask,
But whatever.
First of all, who am *I*?
And secondly,
How do I know these things came to pass?
Well, for better or worse, who am I?
I am Entertainment.
(And the "better or worse" is for you to decide,
Though I will avoid your conclusions for, inside,
My wolf of pride is easily woken
And easily bruised in its fight.)
But despite this,
Perhaps I have made you laugh,
Perhaps I've made you cry,
Perhaps you're bored shitless
And are currently wondering why
You've stuck with this up to now.
(And for those, I thank you for the time you've allowed
And can assure you we are nearly done

And you can soon return to whatever it is
You consider a more worthwhile or fun way
To spend the conscious hours of your time.)
But before I leave you, may you allow me
Just a few more minutes worth of lines
For a simple admission -
One I can no longer hold back,
For, through my telling and recalling,
I have beaten myself into submission
With the club of Hypocrisy.
And, like so often,
Every word spoken is ultimately worthless
If one cannot finish in honesty.
How do I know that such events occurred?
Well, I was there for it all...
And I did nothing...
In favour of curiosity and endings absurd.
For the sake of a story? For the sensation of shock?
For the sake of conversation in shallow-moraled talk?
I don't know. But I saw it all take place...
And did nothing.
I was there when Fear walked into the street,
I was there when he found himself at Lust's tempting feet.
I was there when he crept out of Purity's room,
I raised a glass as he drank himself into his doom.
And I did nothing...
I did nothing but watch with a keen writer's eye
As his marriage to Love rotted in lies,
And I told myself it was not my place to say,
Appealing, *"Who am I to lift rugs where secret stains lay?"*
I knew for months of Purity's child,
I was next door when Fear fled possessed and wild.

I remember the night that Hate was born,
And in the years that came when the underclass formed
Their movements rich in radical reason,
That rose to riots of resentment in the regions,
I did nothing.
I did nothing but watch from balconies of intellectual degree,
Intellectualising and extemporising on the issues of poverty.
I'd make light of problems, then criticise the leaders,
And then sought my inspiration from Beggary's bleeders.
I did nothing.
I watched Hate grow up in the dirt of the slums
As the prelude to all that hate can become
When our actions are no more than well-meaning words
To show that we care while our well-being's preserved;
While we take steps back to see poverty's full scale
Yet never advance to feel the heat of their Hell.
I did nothing.
I remember the night when Purity passed,
I heard of when Hate met Truth at last,
Then I watched a son shoot his father dead
To numb his heart and let his hate spread,
And still, I did nothing
But sigh in solidarity for a stranger's suffering.
I was there when the poor rose to their feet
And demanded respect from the so-called elite.
I was there when Revolution joined hands with Crime
Like long-lost brothers of Poverty's design.
I was there when Protest tipped over the edge
While Chaos and Riot made good their pledge,
And when the daughter of Innocence
Was caught in the crossfire,
Photographed on the ground, bleeding from the head,

EPILOGUE

Still I did nothing.
I watched Reason get lynched by the mob
And crucified on a cross as he begged them stop,
Still I did nothing.
I watched statues fall, I watched leaders get mauled
After mobs smashed windows and scaled palace walls.
And when Revenge was sworn in as leader of the state
And let Greed hold office and let Madness dictate
Their strategy of war,
While nobody knew what the hell was being fought for,
Still I did nothing.
I watched on screens as bombs were dropped
On guiltless lives reimagined as dots,
Still I did nothing.
I watched as we cheapened the price of a life
To a thought in a moment where you don't think twice,
Still I did nothing.
I watched as soldiers from every side
Were subjected to serve in each other's suicide
While, back home, posthumous medals of honour
Were awarded to the lambs we had thrown to the slaughter,
Still, I did nothing
But hope someone else might do something
As I spoke with passion to touch on hearts
And pretend I was somehow playing my part.
I did nothing
But read the news and watch TV,
Dulling my senses to each new atrocity
In the comforting knowledge that I was safe and free...
Until lawless discord came for me in random attack
To recruit one more refugee,
Penniless and possessionless but for the clothes on his back.

And then I ran.
I ran like every other victim of Insanity's command.
And I saw Hate stand with Death in the field,
I saw Confusion flee from all that was real,
I cowered behind Kindness when Compassion wouldn't yield To the threat of a gun,
Before the hope of morality was completely undone.
And I did nothing but run,
Then hid in a truck hoping that no one would come.
And eventually, I sought Love's shelter
With nothing to give in return
But shame.
With all my tepid past words spoken,
In truth, I was part of the silent majority -
In passive sympathy, condoning each brutal atrocity.
I was there when Hate confessed his crimes,
And we all thought back to our younger times,
And it was then I learned
The true weight of my bystanding mind.
I have seen fear ruin love,
I have seen fear breed hate,
I have seen greed breed poverty
And the wars we can create;
And I chose to watch it all through eyes of indifference.

In all the crimes I have witnessed
There is perhaps none more great
Than my own.

The End

Born and raised on the Isle of Arran, off Scotland's west coast, Paul Tinto is an actor and writer based in Glasgow. In front of the camera, his credits include the award-winning TV series *The Crown*, *Outlander*, and *Guilt*, and feature films including *Firebrand*, *Tommy's Honour*, and the BAFTA award-winning *1917*. On stage, Paul's work has taken him all over the UK and beyond, performing in London's West End, Edinburgh's Traverse and Lyceum Theatres, The Manchester Royal Exchange, and The Sheffield Crucible, among others, as well as touring the USA with the National Theatre of Scotland's international hit play, *Black Watch*. In video gaming, Paul can be heard in the current *Final Fantasy VII* trilogy, voicing the fun-loving, fortune-telling cat, Cait Sith!

Trouble In Spiritland is Paul's debut novel.

BVPRI - #0035 - 071024 - C0 - 216/140/9 [11] - CB - 9781738470709 - Matt Lamination